Primitive blaze

"How did we get on to that subject?" he muttered.

"Lovers," she reminded him.

A slash of red speared across his cheekbones. "Then we have comprehensively dismissed that aspect of our association," he stated grimly.

"No, we haven't," Sophie disagreed. "Do you have a lover, Mr. Lombard?"

"I can handle my private life myself, Miss Melville," he bit out cautiously.

"Then I won't cause any jealous scenes or interfere with the passion in your life?" Sophie asked.

"No chance!"

The vehement reply left Sophie with no ground to probe any further. "Oh, good!" she said dismissively, but she wasn't sure if it was good or not. Sophie rather relished the idea of a passionate scene with Jason Lombard.

EMMA DARCY nearly became an actress until her fiancé declared he preferred to attend the theater *with* her. She became a wife and mother. Later, she took up oil painting—unsuccessfully, she remarks. Then she tried architecture, designing the family home in New South Wales. Next came romance writing—"the hardest and most challenging of all the activities," she confesses.

Books by Emma Darcy

HARLEQUIN PRESENTS
1472—THE SEDUCTION OF KEIRA
1496—THE VELVET TIGER
1511—DARK HERITAGE
1519—HEART OF THE OUTBACK
1536—AN IMPOSSIBLE DREAM
1555—THE UPSTAIRS LOVER
1570—NO RISKS, NO PRIZES

HARLEQUIN ROMANCE
2900—BLIND DATE
2941—WHIRLPOOL OF PASSION
3085—PATTERN OF DECEIT

EMMA DARCY

A Very Stylish Affair

Harlequin Books

TORONTO • NEW YORK • LONDON
AMSTERDAM • PARIS • SYDNEY • HAMBURG
STOCKHOLM • ATHENS • TOKYO • MILAN
MADRID • WARSAW • BUDAPEST • AUCKLAND

This book is dedicated to all the wonderful caring
hairdressers who make women look good and feel
good, but especially to Kerry, a truly creative artist,
whose salon, The Cutting Point, at Tumbi Umbi, on
the central coast of New South Wales, is always
cheerful and friendly. Many thanks to Kerry and her
staff for the inspiration and advice given for
A Very Stylish Affair.

Harlequin Presents first edition August 1993
ISBN 0-373-11579-2

A VERY STYLISH AFFAIR

CHAPTER ONE

YOU GET the *real* news at the hairdressers'.

Jason Lombard's mother had been telling him that for so many years, he had come to accept it had a basis of truth. After all, where else could one find out what restaurant was the best value for money, who was divorcing whom, who was cheating on their partners, how good the latest videos were, what shows were worth seeing, the names of tradespeople who were reliable and trustworthy?

That was the short list. There was also the open discussion of social issues, not to mention the dissecting of sensational crimes, critical appraisals on the public behaviour of celebrities and fulsome comment on the television news. Which, of course, was not the *real* news, only a superficial reporting of facts that needed a lot of fleshing out and sorting through of what was not being told.

Jason knew he was about to get some *real* news the moment his mother swept into his office, her hair newly cut, styled and coloured, her blue eyes agleam with recently acquired knowledge and a zeal for sharing it.

"The unemployment problem in Australia is dreadful, Jason," she declared as he rose from his desk to greet her.

"One of the effects of the recession," he remarked non-committally.

"It's worse than the government says it is!" his mother cried in righteous outrage. "For one thing, they don't count the unemployed men who have wives working."

"That relates to social services. The household does have an income and can survive without government help," Jason explained as he moved to meet her for the ritual kiss on the cheek. He smoothly accompanied that with the ritual compliment. "You're looking wonderful, Mother. I like the softer style around your face. Very feminine."

It momentarily distracted her from the burning issue of unemployment. "Thank you, dear. What do you think of the new apricot shade?" She primped and turned around to give him every viewpoint. "I had blonde streaks put through it in case it was too much."

"A delightful variation," he said warmly, knowing it would completely ruin his mother's pleasure in her appearance if he failed to give wholehearted approval.

"I'm so glad you like it." She beamed approval at him until she recalled her mission. "But I didn't come to show off my hair to you. I came to talk to you about the job you advertised. Employers simply aren't giving the unemployed a fair chance, Jason."

Jason had a nasty feeling of premonition as he watched his mother settle herself in a chair, obviously intent on not being shifted or sidetracked from what was on her mind. He resumed his seat behind the desk, knowing only too well that when Kathryn Whitlow had a bee in her bonnet, there was hell to pay one way or another. She might look soft and pliable, but she had the grinding bite of a bulldog when she got her teeth into something.

"I met the loveliest young woman at the salon today," his mother started brightly. "She was having her hair coloured, too, so we had time for a nice long chat. She was feeling really down because she'd just received a letter with another knockback for a job she would have liked."

Since one of his mother's solutions to depression was to change the colour of her hair, Jason could readily understand that the two women would share instant empathy. Very wisely he did not point out that an unemployed person could surely find better use for money than a splash out on vanity. Such a pragmatic remark would only provoke a lecture on male insensitivity to female psychology.

"She talked about all the jobs she had applied for in the last six months," his mother continued, "and not once has she been granted an interview. Not once!"

The injustice of such discrimination rang through her voice, and Jason stirred himself to answer it. "Mother, some jobs draw literally hundreds of applicants in these hard times. An employer cannot afford to spend days or weeks on a series of interviews. It simply isn't productive.''

"So how do you choose whom to see?" his mother demanded.

"By various criteria. Work experience, qualifications..."

"She has work experience and qualifications."

Jason shrugged. "Then others have more. Or have better references."

"But that's only written words on a page. Doesn't the person count for anything?" his mother argued.

"Yes. That's why an employer does hold interviews, Mother," Jason said reasonably.

"How many applicants did you get for the job you advertised?" she fired at him.

"Seventy-three."

"And how many are you going to interview?"

"Seven."

"How long do you spend on an interview?"

"Fifteen minutes is usually enough to tell..."

"Then an extra fifteen minutes isn't going to take up too much of your productive time, Jason," his mother declared triumphantly. "The least you can do is give Sophie Melville a chance instead of putting her on the scrap heap like everyone else. It made me feel terrible when I found out that you were responsible for her disappointment and despair."

Jason gritted his teeth. The nasty premonition was fast becoming unpalatable reality. "I hope you didn't promise her anything, Mother."

Her eyebrows flew up in disdain. "Admit to the person on the receiving end of your blatant and callous insincerity that you were my son? You put me in a very untenable position, Jason."

"I'm sorry, Mother," he soothed, relieved that some sense of discretion had held her sympathy in check.

"How would you feel if you got a letter dashing your hopes that read—" She reached into her handbag and flourished the form letter he had sent out. "'I deeply regret...'" Her blue eyes flashed scorn. "How can you deeply regret an action when you haven't done anything at all?"

"It's merely a polite way—"

"It's obscene, Jason. Dishonest and obscene. And it goes on—"

"Mother, I know what I wrote," Jason cut in curtly. "I sent out sixty-six such letters, each costing me stationery and a forty-five-cent stamp, not to mention the time spent by my secretary. It was, in fact, a courtesy that few employers bother with these days. What do you expect me to write? Tough luck, you're not good enough to make it to the short list?"

It was absolutely rotten luck for him that his mother had been the recipient of a tale of woe from one of the unsuccessful applicants, Jason thought bitterly. Now he was in for a bout of do-gooding interference. He could smell it coming.

"Why wasn't Sophie good enough?"

He heaved an exasperated sigh. "I don't remember."

His mother snorted. "Well, whatever criteria you judged by, you were wrong about her, Jason. It's not her fault that she came home to a recession. That's the government's fault."

"Came home from where?" Jason asked pertinently.

"It's only natural that she should have wanted to visit England. Her parents emigrated from there when she was only a baby. Then it was only sensible to see as much of Europe as she could. That's why she took all those temporary jobs in London, to save the money so she could travel."

Great! thought Jason. No doubt she would be off again to discover Asia or the Americas as soon as she built up enough savings to keep her out of trouble.

"I need someone who will stick with me, Mother," he said, without hope for that vital piece of understanding.

"Jason, you also need someone bright and enterprising." Kathryn Whitlow put on her bulldog face. "I want you to give her a chance."

He closed his eyes, counted to ten, then addressed his mother in a very firm voice. "On average, I do you a favour a month, all of them expensive, but none of them I grudge. Asking me to take on a personal assistant, sight unseen, whom I have to live with day in and day out, is going too far, Mother.''

"I didn't say you had to take her without seeing her first. Obviously you have to give her an interview or it will look fishy. I wouldn't want her to think she didn't get the job on her own merits. Call in your secretary and I'll dictate the letter.''

"I prefer to dictate my own letters, Mother,'' Jason said resentfully.

"Then I'll listen while you do it. Make sure you get the wording nice and right. And it will have to be sent right away in order to catch the mail. Poor Sophie will be spending a miserable weekend as it is. At least she'll have good news on Monday.''

His clients trusted him to get the wording right on million-dollar contracts. Jason prided himself on using language effectively. With care, conciseness and simplicity. But there was no point in arguing with his mother. She had even scorned his legal expertise and drafted her own will.

An interview, Jason reasoned, was only fifteen minutes. The most economic course of action was clear. He called his secretary, asked her to bring in Sophie Melville's application, then smiled at his mother with every appearance of compliance to her wishes.

"I'll give her the chance to impress me, Mother,'' he said indulgently, "but if she doesn't suit my requirements, nothing will induce me to take her on. Fair enough?''

"Really, Jason," his mother chided, her eyes glowing with brilliant satisfaction, "as if I wouldn't know the kind of person who would suit you! Sophie will be perfect in every way. She has the most glorious head of hair...."

CHAPTER TWO

SOPHIE CLENCHED HER HANDS as the receptionist continued to stare at her hair.

"Sophie Melville," she repeated in a small, tight voice. "For an interview with Mr. Lombard. I have a letter of confirmation...."

The receptionist finally wrenched her gaze down. "Miss Melville," she echoed distractedly, checking the appointment list. There were eight names on it, Sophie noted, as she watched the receptionist's pen run slowly down to the last of them. "Yes. You're here. If you'll take a seat..." She nodded to where four women were already waiting.

"Thank you," said Sophie with heartfelt relief. The letter had not been some mistake. She was definitely expected for an interview. The miracle of a second chance was indeed a reality.

She swung around and met four similar stares, all glued to her hair. Sophie flashed a false bright smile at the women who were undoubtedly competing for the same plum job. Her smile was not returned. They looked away dismissively, certain this newcomer could not possibly be any threat to their chances.

Sophie sat down, fighting an abject wave of despair. Maybe Jason Lombard liked red hair. It might not count against her at all. She had to keep thinking positively, settle her nerves, prepare the answers that would make him see her in the light of a very useful person to have at his side. Surely that was the most important consideration.

But she had the sinking feeling luck was against her. It was a cruel turn of fate that Jason Lombard's secretary had slipped up in sending her the initial rejection letter. If the correct one had arrived on Friday morning, she never would have agreed to being Mia's model for the hairdressing competition. Her hair would still be an ordinary brown and she could have wound it into a professional-looking topknot.

It was the sense of no-one wanting her as she was that had made her susceptible to throwing her cap over the windmill, so to speak. After the mail had come on Friday, she truly hadn't cared what wild experiment Mia wanted to try with her hair. Anything was better than moping over the series of choices that had inadvertently led to her unemployable status. Not that she regretted the experience of seeing all she could of the other side of the world, but all those different jobs hardly made her look like a stable person. Neither did the colour of her hair!

While she couldn't begrudge Mia the first prize she had won, no-one in his or her right mind would imagine this vivid flame was natural. The technical term for it, Mia had told her, was dark blonde with a copper-red reflect. The result was positively iridescent, high-lighted by the thickly layered concoction of ringlets cut into a wild sunburst effect. The judges of the competition had declared Mia's bold creation "fantastic," and they were dead right. It was so fantastic it turned heads everywhere.

Which might have been fine if Sophie were being interviewed for a secretarial position in a modelling agency, but Jason Lombard was a lawyer, and lawyers were notoriously conservative. Sophie did her best to console herself with the thought that Jason Lombard was not an ordinary lawyer.

Many of his clients were flamboyant people, top golfers and tennis stars and the more durable personalities in television and radio. He couldn't possibly be like the stuffy men in the firm of lawyers where she had once worked. He wasn't part of the legal establishment that revolved around the courts, either. He had a reputation of settling in his clients' best interests without recourse to the judicial system. Which saved everyone a lot of money.

And undoubtedly earned him a lot, Sophie thought, her gaze wandering around the professional elegance of the reception room. Lombard and Associates occupied the whole top floor of this prestigious office building, right in the heart of the business sector of North Sydney. With its sweeping views over the harbour and the city, such a position had to cost a pretty penny.

There was no expense spared on furnishings, either. Thick grey carpet, black leather armchairs, lithographs on the wall in black frames, chrome and glass tables, potted plants displaying a lush growth of greenery... Everything quiet and restrained, Sophie realised, her stomach knotting up again. There was not one splash of bright colour anywhere!

It didn't mean Jason Lombard didn't have a personal leaning towards vivid colours, Sophie hastily assured herself. A reception room was for the benefit of other people, and it had probably been designed by an interior decorator specifically to ease unquiet minds. For all she knew, Jason Lombard could harbour a private passion for red.

Sophie surreptitiously appraised her competitors. They all had one thing in common. A quiet appearance. Professional suits, black or grey. Soft blouses, cream, white, dusty pink. One natural blonde and three natural brunettes. Stylish haircuts, easily maintained. Subtle make-up. Silver or gold jewellery.

Well, she certainly stood out from the crowd, Sophie thought, determinedly making that a positive thought. The brightness of her hair had demanded a matching flame lipstick, and then she had been forced to emphasise her blue eyes to balance her royal blue suit. Unlike the black and grey suits, which seemed designed to minimise femininity, Sophie's suit faithfully hugged the hourglass curves of her figure and did not allow for a blouse at all. Nevertheless, it was a good linen suit and there was no reason for her to feel self-conscious in it.

She was sure she was capable of handling the job. That was the main thing. The trick was to convince Jason Lombard she was the best. Her mind was very busy running through possibilities as she waited for her turn to impress.

He gave each woman exactly fifteen minutes, Sophie noted. She could read neither failure nor triumph on their faces as they emerged from their interviews. Their composure was enviable. Sophie knew it was going to be hard to match it. If she didn't clinch this job, she had nothing to fall back on. Yet she could not afford to reveal her inner desperation. Desperate people didn't get hired for positions that required unflappable poise and self-control.

No-one else joined the group during the hour she waited, so there must have been other interviews before she arrived, Sophie reasoned. That matched with the three names that had been ticked off at the top of the receptionist's list. She was the last candidate.

Lucky last, she fiercely recited to herself when she finally took the fateful walk into the presence of the man who would inevitably brighten or darken her future. She was concentrating so hard on all the answers she had prepared she momentarily forgot about her hair.

Until he stared at it.

He was standing beside his desk, ready to extend a courteous greeting, but good manners deserted him in the face of Sophie's flaming sunburst of ringlets. It wasn't simply a matter of him looking stunned for a second or two. He stared so long a glazed look came into his eyes.

"Dear God! What have we here?" he murmured.

Sophie's bravely constructed composure was shot to pieces. Her nerves jangled into painful knots. Her heart cramped, then pumped overtime, pouring a wave of heat up her neck to suffuse her cheeks with a burning brightness that undoubtedly matched her hair. Her mind wilted into limp defeat before a word was uttered. Only a spark of pride remained, urging her to do something, anything, to persuade him into a reappraisal.

"Mr. Lombard—" she forced from her throat that had gone as dry as bleached bones "—you've just made a snap judgement about me. You don't believe I'm suitable for the position you advertised. I'm going to prove that judgement wrong. I want you to start reassessing now. Give me any test you like and I'll pass it. I'm fast, efficient and effective."

It was amazing what desperation could do when unleashed. Sophie had no idea where those words had come from, but they succeeded in focussing Jason Lombard's eyes on hers.

His mouth slowly quirked into a derisive little smile. "Miss . . . Melville."

The pause in between the pronouncement of her name was dreadful, as though he had forgotten it, or wanted to forget it. Sophie thought she might as well walk out now for all the hope she had of getting the job, but a wave of stubbornness insisted she hold her ground, at least for the same amount of time that had been allotted to the others.

"I'm sure you're a busy person, Mr. Lombard. So am I," she lied without batting an eyelash. "You must have a list of questions and a set of answers, against which you will match my replies. It will be much more straightforward if you simply tell me your requirements and I'll give you my rating on them."

That raised his eyebrows.

Sophie brazened out his surprise with her brightest smile. "Shall we sit down and get on with it?"

Without waiting for his reply she walked over to the chair obviously set in front of his desk for the interviewees. Having seated herself with all the poise she could muster, she met his riveted gaze with a challenging lift of her eyebrows. He gave a bemused shake of his head, then walked slowly around his desk and settled himself in the high-backed leather chair that spelled out who was the boss.

It gave Sophie a few moments to make her appraisal of him. Jason Lombard was much younger than she had anticipated, or perhaps he only looked younger. Between thirty and forty was a grey area for men, and sometimes their prime could last to forty-five before the aging process caught up with them. This man was definitely in his prime.

He was tall and broad-shouldered enough to lend an impressive elegance to the superbly tailored three-piece suit he wore. Definitely a European style, probably French or Italian. The fabric had the sheen of some expensive silk mixture. Very classy. The silvery-grey colour matched his silvery-grey eyes, but there were no silvery-grey strands in his jet-black hair yet. He was quite handsome in a mature way. Good bones, Sophie decided. He could be very attractive if he had a nice smile.

He didn't smile.

He opened a wooden box on his desk, removed a set of darts, swivelled his chair around to face the wall and started hurling the darts at the dartboard that hung there. "Have you ever hit a bullseye, Miss Melville?" he asked.

"Frequently. High distinction in darts, Mr. Lombard," she replied pertly, determined not to let him throw her with any diversionary tactics he might employ.

"Blast! Missed again," he muttered. None of the darts were even close to the bullseye. He swung to face her, some private amusement lurking in his eyes. "All right, Miss Melville. We'll conduct the interview your way."

Her brash boldness had paid off, Sophie thought, much encouraged.

"Let's commence with temperament," he continued. "I need someone who'll remain bright and even-tempered. I can't stand surly moody people who brood over imagined slights or bring their personal troubles to work with them."

"Mr. Lombard, I shall scintillate through your day. You could not find anyone brighter."

He looked at her hair, passed a hand over his eyes, rose from his chair and collected the darts from the board. He had an evil glint in his eyes when he swung around to return to his chair. "What about female problems?" he asked silkily.

A trick question, Sophie thought. If she didn't admit to them he might accuse her of being unfeminine. If she did admit to them, he might exaggerate them into something he could hold against her.

His face wore an air of satisfaction as though he was certain he had her cornered. It was perfectly plain to Sophie that no matter what she said or did, Jason Lombard did not want to give her this job. To give herself a chance, she had to pull out all the stops.

She waited until he resumed his seat, then leaned forward, placed her forearm on his desk and lowered her voice to draw him towards her. "Can we be truly confidential, Mr. Lombard?"

He leaned forward in ready response. "By all means," he agreed.

She edged closer to him, lowered her voice even further. "I'll control my female problems if you'll control your male problems."

"Really?" He displayed an eagerness to hear more, his face almost meeting hers. He wasn't easily fazed, Sophie thought. "To what male problems do you refer?" he asked, eyeballing her with avid interest.

Sophie eyeballed him right back. "Men who think themselves irresistible, powerful and prestigious," she whispered with husky suggestiveness. "Men who believe they have the divine right of kings for the laying on of hands. Men who see a woman's body as a playground especially designed for their pleasure. Does that get across the problems I mean, Mr. Lombard?"

"Interesting," he breathed, then rocked back in his chair looking poleaxed. "I'll try for a triple twenty," he muttered, swivelling his seat ninety degrees.

He hurled a dart, which travelled end over end, hit the board fin first and clattered to the floor. He was the worst dart player Sophie had ever seen.

"Missed again," he said. He appeared quite glum for a moment, but when he turned to her he had a bright, scheming look on his face. "You asked for a test. I'll give you a test."

Sophie's heart sank. He was sure to ask for the impossible. Something like reciting back ten telephone numbers, or typing two hundred and fifty words a minute into a computer, or spelling that awful Latin legal terminology that lawyers were so fond of.

His eyes noted her momentary discomfiture and gleamed with rich satisfaction. "The Sullivan wrangle," he said. "Give me your considered opinion of its present position."

Relief surged through Sophie. The scandalous Sullivan affair had been thoroughly discussed at the hairdressing salon on Friday. There was absolutely nothing that she didn't know about it. "Blood on the floor," she tossed back at her inquisitor with supreme confidence.

The dart he held poised in his hand, ready to throw, was not given flight. He swung to face her, his hand thumping on the desk and inadvertently driving the steel point of the dart through the leather writing pad and into the wood beneath.

"You've ruined your dart," she said, feeling enormously pleased with herself. She must have hit a nerve.

He ruefully removed the dart and threw it nonchalantly halfway across the room into a wastepaper basket. It went in. Which had to be a fluke, Sophie reasoned. He couldn't have done it if he'd really tried.

"Now," he said. "What do you mean, blood on the floor?"

Sophie recited the consensus reached by the hairdressers and their patrons. "The Sullivans don't want to settle. The original problem's been forgotten. They're out to do as much hurt and harm to each other as they can. Going for the jugular, regardless of how much they'll hurt themselves. It's bound to be a field day for the lawyers and the newspapers when they go to court."

"How would you stop them from going to court?"

Sophie had the answer to that, too. The solution at the salon had been unanimous. "Stick them down on an island in the middle of an ocean and make them talk to each other."

His eyes flickered. "Like where?" he asked.

That wasn't so simple. An exact location hadn't been discussed, let alone decided upon. Then she remembered the little old lady who was having her hair permed. She had been enthusing about her recent vacation on one of the Tahitian islands. It had sounded absolutely idyllic. If she could only remember the name...

"Bora Bora," Sophie recalled triumphantly.

"Hmm," said Jason Lombard, settling back into his chair with a brooding air.

There was a long nerve-racking silence.

"Did I pass the test with distinction?" Sophie finally had to ask.

The only reply was a sort of rumbling growl.

"Do I get the job?" she persisted.

Jason Lombard was used to thinking quickly and making fast decisions. Sophie Melville was hopelessly unsuitable, yet she did have a certain individual elan. In a class of her own. Although he'd hate to have to define that class to anyone else. Her crowning glory was more than enough to freeze all reasonable thought processes.

Her solution to the Sullivan wrangle had an appealing animal charm. Whenever he talked to those two, he felt a compelling urge to pick both of them up by the scruff of the neck and shake them hard.

His eyes flickered over the woman sitting opposite him, waiting impatiently for his answer. Hopeless. Utterly hopeless. She would raise eyebrows so far that his sanity would be in question if he hired her as his personal assistant.

On the other hand, if they were out of the country, she could be useful to him. And it was always possible to get rid of somebody he didn't really want. His mother would climb off his back if he gave her perfect protégée a chance. He rather liked the idea of killing two birds with one stone.

"Let us consult the omens," he said, rocking forward to duplicate the mood of confidentiality that Sophie Melville had drawn him into before. A pay back was definitely in order. Jason prided himself on always having the edge with unpredictability. Creative solutions were meat and drink to him.

Sophie regarded him with deep suspicion. She leaned her arm on the desk again, determined to bring him to the point. "What omens?" she demanded.

"In ancient times, before any major venture was embarked upon, the omens were always consulted to see if there would be a favourable outcome," he intoned gravely. "Let's see if luck is on our side."

"What do you have in mind?" Sophie bit out, sensing another diversionary tactic was on the way.

"I'll give you a month's trial if the omens are right. I'm going to throw two darts. If one hits the triple twenty and the second hits the bullseye, then fate favours the arrangement."

"Oh, no!" she groaned. On that premise fate couldn't be more horribly stacked against her.

"Simple!" he cried, a truly wicked twinkle in his eyes. "Let's see where we stand." Then with barely a glance at the board to take any reasonably accurate aim, he hurled off the first dart.

"That's totally unfair..." Sophie's anguished protest trailed into sheer disbelief as the dart landed fair, smack between the wires and right in the centre of the twenty.

"I've done it! I've done it!" he crowed.

"You did it!" Sophie gasped. It was a great shot, worthy of a champion.

"Now for the bullseye," he said.

"No!" she shrieked, not trusting him to fluke a repeat performance.

He stood up, his eyes aglow, his hand quivering. He nearly dropped the dart in his excitement.

"Wait a minute!" Sophie commanded.

"May the omens go with you," he spoke to the dart.

"It's my turn!" Sophie shouted, knowing that her only chance was to take control of this outrageous game instantly. "A joint venture is a joint venture, Mr. Lombard. It's *my* turn with the dart."

While he was still cogitating this challenge, Sophie marched around the desk and snatched the dart out of his hand. With a speed that left him standing, she walked straight to the board, drew her arm back and thrust the dart deeply into the bullseye.

"There!" she said with satisfaction. "The first in the triple twenty, the second in the bullseye."

"That's not fair!" he protested this time. "You didn't throw it."

"I didn't say I was going to throw it." She swung around to face him, her eyes lit with triumph. "I made no claim whatsoever on how I would proceed. Luck is what you make it, in my book."

"You said you had a high distinction in darts," he argued, clearly put out by her spoiling action.

"That was when I was eight years old. Now, do I get the job, Mr. Lombard?"

A reluctant spark of admiration glinted in his eyes. His mouth curled self-mockingly. "Starting tomorrow, you're on a month's trial," he conceded.

Sophie clasped her hands in an ecstasy of relief and delight. "Oh, thank you, Mr. Lombard. I'll be perfect for you. You'll see. Thank you, thank you, thank you."

She was employed, her mind sang. Employed in a plum job! A kind of effervescent madness seized her, and her feet danced right over to the man who had granted her a chance, and her arms threw themselves around his neck, and her lips planted a profusion of grateful kisses all around his jawline.

"Miss Melville! Control these female urges!" Jason Lombard said sternly. "Decorum is an essential requirement for this position."

Sophie collected herself and drew back, bestowing her best beautiful smile on him to show how ready she was to please. "Mr. Lombard, starting tomorrow, I shall be the quintessence of decorum. And anything else you require. What time do you want me here?''

"Nine o'clock. And I abhor unpunctuality."

"Oh, so do I, Mr. Lombard," Sophie trilled, whirling to her chair to pick up her handbag. "I won't waste a minute of your time. Not now, or ever. And thank you once again for giving me a chance."

Jason's gaze was drawn to the jaunty swing of her shapely hips as she walked quickly to the door. He could still feel the soft feminine squash of her full breasts against his chest. Desirable, he thought. Dangerously desirable. He wondered if there was scarlet lipstick all around his jaw.

She threw a dazzling smile over her shoulder as she opened the door. "Punctuality and decorum," she recited in a delightfully bubbly fashion, her vivid blue eyes throwing off more sparks than her outrageously fire-red hair.

With her exit finally effected, Jason drew out a handkerchief and thoughtfully rubbed it over his chin. Maybe he had overdone it with a month's trial. Sophie Melville could present him with some severe male problems. He would have to take care, a great deal of care, to avoid that.

Because she really wasn't suitable.

CHAPTER THREE

SOPHIE WAS RIDING A HIGH for the rest of the day. Not only had she finally escaped from the depressing ranks of the unemployed, she had a marvellous feeling this job was just right for her. In the seven years of her working life Sophie had never once felt that, despite the variety of positions she had held.

Sometimes, in the temporary jobs she had taken, she had been invited to stay on and become a permanent employee, but she had never been tempted to take up the option. Perhaps the lure of foreign places had blocked her mind to possibilities, but Sophie didn't think so. There hadn't been anything uniquely special for her in those jobs.

Not like with Jason Lombard.

Working for him was going to be the most exciting challenge of her life. His tests and tricks and tactics compelled her to think as she had never thought before, and it was exhilarating to know she had got the better of him today, making him change his mind about his initial judgement of her. She could hardly wait for tomorrow.

The afternoon sped by in the joy of spreading the good news. Mia instantly took credit for making Sophie look outstanding. Her parents were delighted to hear their daughter had finally found employment in Sydney. There was nothing on offer for young people in the country town where they lived. Now they could stop worrying about Sophie.

At six o'clock, Mia came bursting into the small flat she and Sophie shared. Her short blonde bob had been clipped much shorter during the day and was now a gleaming copper. "I decided red is a lucky colour," she declared, twirling around their tiny kitchen to show off the new look.

"Very chic." It was Sophie's standard response to all of Mia's frequent changes of style and colour. She tactfully refrained from mentioning that linking red with luck was highly questionable.

"And now begins the celebration!" Mia cried, producing a bottle of white wine from her bag.

"Oh, Mia! You shouldn't have! I owe you too much already," Sophie chided, but her pleasure in her friend's generosity could not be denied.

"Rubbish! After you rang and told me of your brilliant handling of the interview and getting a month's trial out of Jason Lombard, some carousing was definitely in order. What are you cooking?"

"It's only a chicken stir-fry."

"Smells great! Anything that somebody else cooks for me always tastes delicious," Mia rattled on at top speed. Words spilled from her lips with machine-gun rapidity. "And I've got a delicious piece of news for an appetiser. I've been dying to tell you ever since I heard, but I made myself wait for this moment.''

Mia's hands were as busy as her tongue. The cork came out of the wine bottle with a loud plop. ''Geronimo!'' she cried merrily, grabbed two glasses off the shelf near the refrigerator and filled them in a trice. She handed one to Sophie then lifted the other in a toast. ''Success! How sweet it is!''

''It certainly is!'' Sophie heartily agreed. She took a sip of wine then asked, ''So what's the news?''

''You'll never guess!'' Mia's bright brown eyes danced with gossipy glee. ''After you rang me, I was so excited for you, I was nattering away to one of my clients about your successful interview, and she said—''

A pause for dramatic affect. Mia adored making the most of every story, and she was very good at it.

''Go on,'' Sophie eagerly encouraged.

Mia's finely plucked eyebrows waggled up and down. ''—your new boss, Jason Lombard, had a long-standing affair with Gail Kingston before she married Randy Sullivan. What do you think of that connection?''

For some reason Sophie inwardly shied away from it, as though the connection was distasteful. Yet history was history. It would be unnatural for a man as clever and good-looking as Jason Lombard not to have had various involvements with women.

''I guess it accounts for his interest in what's happening to them now,'' Sophie said slowly.

"And maybe accounts for why he's never married," Mia speculated, hitching herself onto a stool and kicking her shoes off. "According to my source, he hasn't been seriously linked with any other woman."

Sophie gave the fried rice a stir. "Well, if it was a long-standing affair, he had plenty of time to marry her if that's what he wanted."

"Probably didn't suit at the time. Both of them with busy separate careers," Mia reasoned. "Then Randy swooped onto the scene and carried her off to stardom with him. And the titillating part is, Jason Lombard was best man at their wedding."

Sophie frowned. "Then he must be friends with both of them."

"Mmm... Interesting, isn't it?" Mia's eyes sparkled at the possibility of more juicy scandal. "Do you suppose he's doing some counselling and consoling with gorgeous Gail right now?"

A picture of the strikingly beautiful Gail Sullivan flashed into Sophie's mind. She had long, straight, honey-coloured hair. Natural and elegant. Somehow that image tarnished the bright shine of Sophie's day.

"I've no idea," she murmured, discomfited by the memory of Jason Lombard brooding over her solution to the Sullivan problem. "He made no personal reference to her," she added to kill that line of speculation. She didn't like it, and she didn't want Mia to pursue it.

It took Sophie quite a while to figure out why she
didn't like it. The question nagged at the edge of her
mind through the celebration dinner and was still
nagging hours later as she lay in the dark of the narrow little bedroom she sublet from Mia. When the
answer finally hit her, she felt quite shocked by it.

How could she possibly consider Jason Lombard
hers? They had only met today, for heaven's sake!
Apart from which, he might be up to ten years older
than her. Virtually a different generation. Which was
fine for an employer, but she had to be off her brain
to feel attracted to the man, or to want him to feel attracted to her.

It simply wasn't suitable.

It could play havoc with her concentration on the
job, and she needed the job.

Sophie squirmed as she remembered almost smoth-
ering him with kisses. He must have wondered what on
earth he had got himself into in giving her a month's
trial. It had been such a mad thing for her to do. But
then, he had been just as mad with his omens and dart
throwing.

She smothered the grin that erupted from the sweet
recollection of beating him at his own game. Strict
decorum from now on, she promised herself. Above
all, she had to control any female urges around him.
If Gail Sullivan represented Jason Lombard's taste in
women, he wasn't about to see his new personal assistant as a woman he wanted to invite into his private

life. There was absolutely no sense in thinking of him in any other light than employer.

Sophie carried that firm resolution to work with her the next morning. From where she lived at Lindfield, it was a twenty-minute train trip to North Sydney. Nevertheless, she took no risks on punctuality. She caught an early train and arrived at her place of business with fifteen minutes to spare.

The receptionist arrived at the same time. Her name was Cheryl Hughes, and while she still seemed to be continually distracted by Sophie's hair, she kindly showed Sophie to the office she was to occupy.

Predictably enough, it had a connecting door to Mr. Lombard's office, and was comprehensively equipped with every aid for communication purposes. Sophie extracted some other important information from Cheryl, so that when Jason Lombard arrived at precisely nine o'clock, she was in the act of placing a cup of coffee on his desk, made exactly to his liking.

She gave him a bright, welcoming smile. "Good morning, Mr. Lombard."

It caught him by surprise. He stared at her, not for as long as he had yesterday, but long enough for Sophie to feel her heart hop, skip and jump. He looked very manly in his grey suit.

"Good morning, Miss Melville," he finally returned, then closed the door behind him with slow deliberation. "Kind of you to bring me coffee," he said as he moved forward. "Please make yourself a cup and join me. Then we'll get started on the business of the day.''

Smooth, pleasant, taking command with an effortless ease that shrugged off any second thoughts he might have had about giving her a trial run. Sophie released the breath she had been holding and flashed him another bright smile. "Thank you. I'll be right back, Mr. Lombard.''

Decorum, she reminded herself sternly, controlling the urge to rush, and forcing herself to walk away from him with conscious grace and perfect deportment. She could feel him watching her and hoped he appreciated the efforts she was making to fulfil his requirements. Certainly he could find nothing objectionable about her navy skirt and white blouse. They were nothing if not conservative. And decorous.

He was seated behind his desk when she returned. Sophie was conscious of his gaze fastened on her all the way back to him, but she didn't once rattle the cup in its saucer. Which was a major feat, considering the jittery state of her nerves.

He waited until she drew up a chair and sat down opposite him before offering an encouraging little smile. "Now, Miss Melville, let's establish some ground rules for your position as my personal assistant.''

Sophie flipped open her notebook and poised her pen ready to write.

"These are unwritten rules, Miss Melville.''

She looked up into eyes that sliced into her with the precision of a scalpel.

"Break them at your peril," he intoned in a soft, infinitely dangerous voice.

Sophie took a deep breath. "I'll do my best to remember them, Mr. Lombard."

"Better than best. You will remember them, Miss Melville. At all times."

"Yes, sir."

"First and foremost, your position is one of utmost confidentiality. You will not breathe a word of my business to anyone unless I instruct you to do so. Then you will carry out my instructions to the letter. Have you got that, Miss Melville?"

"Confidentiality," she repeated, nodding quickly for extra emphasis.

"You do not leak information. You do not gossip. You respect my clients' privacy with the fervour of a nun under a vow of silence. Anything you hear or read in this office stays in this office. Do I make myself clear, Miss Melville?"

His voice was like a whip, and Sophie felt the lash of it on her conscience. But he had not put an embargo of silence on yesterday's interview. He could hardly blame her for talking about that. "My lips are sealed from this moment on, Mr. Lombard," she fervently promised him.

"Above all," he continued bitingly, "you will keep my name and my business, both professional and private, out of the endless chatter that undoubtedly goes on at the hairdressing salon you frequent, Miss Melville."

There was nothing Sophie could do to stop the rush of hot shaming colour to her cheeks. But Jason Lombard couldn't possibly know about her showing his initial rejection letter to the sympathetic lady who was seated next to her in the salon on Friday. And he couldn't know about her association with Mia, either.

Yet there was a horribly knowing look in the steely grey eyes observing the progress of her fiery blush. Sophie thought she would hate to be a witness being cross-examined by him. He was sharp and shrewd and didn't miss a trick. But since her job depended on outfacing him, she would outface him if it killed her.

"Check list," she said in a quick, snappy voice. "Strict adherence to holy orders. Nun's vows. Walls of privacy kept intact. Silence at hairdressers'. Under penalty of death." She projected limpid innocence into her blue eyes. "Does that cover everything, Mr. Lombard?"

"Admirably, Miss Melville," he said dryly.

"Anything else?" she asked.

"Do you have a current passport?"

"Yes, Mr. Lombard."

"Do you live with anyone?"

"Yes."

"Man or woman?"

"Woman."

"Friend or lover?"

"Really!" Sophie protested. "That's a bit personal, isn't it?"

He shrugged. "No offense meant."

"You ask all your employees about their living arrangements?"

"What I am trying to elicit, Miss Melville, is whether or not you can accompany me at a moment's notice. I'm prepared to give consideration to the fact that my requirements could cause personal difficulties in your private life. If you have a lover, male or female..."

"I don't!" Sophie declared with some vehemence. "And you?"

"What?"

"Well, I ought to know what I'm travelling with, and you brought up the subject," Sophie argued.

His eyebrows shot up. "You're asking me if I have a lover?"

"Male or female? There must be some reason that you're not married. You're fairly old...."

He stiffened. "I am thirty-three, Miss Melville."

"Oh! Is that all?" Sophie breathed, absurdly pleased that he was only eight years older. It wasn't so much of a gap to cross.

"And I do not consider I'm over the hill as far as women are concerned," he bit out as though he would like to sink his teeth into her for having the temerity to suggest he couldn't get himself a woman whenever he wanted. "There are reasons for not being married...."

"Like what?" Sophie asked curiously. It would be nice if she could get the Gail Sullivan matter cleared up.

"Like being too busy building a business to give a marriage the time it needs if it's to work," he grated.

"Okay. Fair enough," she soothed. Mia could be right about busy careers.

His eyes glittered over her in such a hot, pointed fashion that Sophie almost squirmed in her seat. The challenge to his manhood had certainly stirred a response in him. He looked as though he would like to throw her down on the floor, rip off her clothes and comprehensively show her the full extent of his maleness.

Sophie found it such a tantalising thought that her breasts started tingling with excitement. She felt her nipples tighten and quickly picked up her cup of coffee, holding it with both hands to sip at it, thereby covering up any telltale response to the primitive blaze of desire she had unwittingly provoked.

His hand jerked out for his cup and he grimaced in annoyance as he wrenched his gaze from her and glared at the coffee she had made for him. "How did we get onto that subject?" he muttered.

"Lovers," she reminded him.

A slash of red speared across his cheekbones. "Then we have comprehensively dismissed that aspect of our association," he stated grimly.

"No, we haven't," Sophie disagreed. "*Do you* have a lover, Mr. Lombard?"

"I can handle my private life myself, Miss Melville," he bit out caustically.

"Then I won't cause any jealous scenes or interfere with the passions in your life?" Sophie asked.

"No chance!"

The vehement reply left Sophie with no ground to probe any further. "Oh, good!" she said dismissively, but she wasn't sure if it was good or not. She rather relished the idea of a passionate scene with Jason Lombard.

They drank their coffee in a silence that twanged with tension. Suddenly they were no longer employer and employee but man and woman, intensely aware of their own and each other's sexuality. Sophie couldn't help exulting that Jason Lombard was attracted to her after all. If only physically. Who knew what else could develop between them in the month stretching ahead?

Maybe it wasn't so unsuitable.

Thirty-three was not too old for her. There was a lot to be said for maturity and experience. Nevertheless, as pleasant as it was to daydream of having Jason Lombard as hers, Sophie was still conscious of not doing anything to jeopardise her job with him.

He finished his coffee, cleared his throat and made a curt announcement. "This is your first assignment. You are to obtain all the necessary information to get from here to Bora Bora and back again. Flight times, flight connections..."

"Ah! The Sullivan wrangle!" said Sophie with deep satisfaction. "That shows you have an open mind."

He winced. "Also the availability of rooms at the Hotel Bora Bora."

"They're not rooms," she said. "They're *farés*."

He sighed deeply. "All right. The availability of *farés*."

"You'll want them on the beach front, won't you? More romantic that way. And right next to each other. That should help." Sophie was so pleased that he wanted Gail Sullivan back with her husband, she was delighted to help in any way she could.

Unaccountably his voice held irritation as he dictated. "The availability of three *farés* on the beach front, all next to each other, at the Hotel Bora Bora."

Marvellous, Sophie thought. One for the Sullivans, one for Jason Lombard and one for herself. "We'll have to get moving on the visas, as well," she said. "I'll do yours at the same time as mine."

He stood up in a very aggressive mode, white knuckles pressing on his desk. "Who said you were going?"

Sophie looked at him in mild reproof. "In a matter as delicate as this, how can you do without me? And anyway, it was my idea in the first place." Besides, why would he ask about her passport if he didn't intend taking her?

He sat down very slowly and appeared to have a gnawing desire to chew his lower lip. It took him some time to formulate what he wanted to say. "You are a very annoying and exasperating woman, Miss Melville," he finally clipped out.

"I'll put that on the unwritten rules list. Not to annoy or exasperate," Sophie said soothingly.

His mouth thinned into a grimly constrained line. His eyes glittered at her with a hint of lurking vengeance. "Are you prepared for anything, Miss Melville?"

"Certainly, Mr. Lombard."

"Then remember, at all times, that I'm the one in charge of this operation. I don't want you leaping six steps ahead of me. You follow orders."

"I'll do my best to stay behind you, Mr. Lombard," Sophie assured him earnestly.

He breathed in and out like a dragon ready to attack, but he spoke with controlled precision. "Your orders are that today's assignment must be carried out with the utmost discretion. You bring the information I've asked for to me. Then I'll do the necessary bookings as and when I choose. Use discretion and tact, Miss Melville. I want no connection made to this office or me. You must pretend that you personally want the information. Is that understood?"

"Yes, Mr. Lombard. Discretion and tact, as well. No problem."

"Then go find a travel agency, Miss Melville, and get moving on it."

"Yes, sir. Full speed, no brake."

She leapt to her feet and gathered the coffee cups from the desk. Images of sharing a tropical paradise with Jason Lombard flashed across Sophie's mind. Pleasurable anticipation zinged through her heart.

While she had to adjust her thinking to stay behind his planning speed, she could certainly put an oar in the works if Gail Sullivan looked like being the centre of his attention. All in all, the future was definitely bright.

Jason Lombard watched the fascinating undulation of feminine movement as Sophie Melville sallied off to do his bidding. With a supreme act of will he lifted his gaze to the fiery halo of ridiculous ringlets. *Keep looking at her hair,* he sternly advised himself. A woman with hair like that could not hold any fascination for him.

He frowned and shook his head over the incredible agility of her mind. Feed her one piece of information and she leapt ahead to devastating conclusions. And those vivid blue eyes were an absolute mantrap, the way they kept changing with intriguing expressions. Sophie Melville was fast becoming a very disturbing element in his life. But if he kept looking at her hair, that would surely provide safe anchorage.

CHAPTER FOUR

OVER THE NEXT FEW DAYS, Sophie showed Jason Lombard how efficient and effective she could be as his personal assistant. Collecting and collating the travel data for the Bora Bora operation was a snap for her, and she knew precisely how to cut administrative red tape when it came to getting visas. With the quick adaptability learnt from taking up many temporary jobs, mastering the office system didn't present any problems to her. The one problem she did have was with the rest of the staff.

Everyone did a double take on meeting her. Associates and their secretaries alike stared incredulously at her hair as though she were some freak from a circus. Sophie's patience was sorely tried before she could get them to concentrate on the business in hand. She resorted to using Mr. Lombard's name frequently and emphatically to focus attention on what needed to be done.

What annoyed her most was that Jason Lombard seemed to have developed a fixation on her hair, as well. Every time she proved herself capable of delivering whatever he asked of her, brightly, correctly and with all his unwritten rules religiously adhered to, he frowned at her hair as though she were deliberately using a flaming helmet to camouflage a creditable brain.

He did it once too often on Friday afternoon.

"It's really brown," Sophie said, when he looked at her hair instead of being properly impressed by the prodigious amount of work she had completed for him.

He lowered a blank uncomprehending gaze to hers.

"I was a model for a hairdressing competition last Sunday. That's why it's like this," Sophie explained. "It would damage my hair if I had it stripped. So I can't change it back from red for another five weeks."

"By then it won't matter," he muttered, and dropped his gaze to the sheaf of perfectly typed pages she had delivered to him.

Sophie wasn't sure what he meant by that remark, but she didn't like the sound of it. She took a deep breath, marched around to his side of the desk and jabbed a finger past his nose and onto the printed pages.

"This is what I expect to be assessed on, Mr. Lombard. Not the colour or style of my hair. Which, I might add, won the competition. However, since you're only a man, I understand that this is a field of creative art you may not be readily comfortable with."

He rocked back in his chair and glowered at her. "It is very bright, Miss Melville. And distracting."

"What would you like me to do? Stuff my hair under a wig or a scarf for the duration? Wear a nun's veil

in keeping with the vow of silence? Dress in pur-
dah?'' Her eyes glittered their challenge, even as she
smiled brightly to show how even-tempered she was
about it.

He grimaced. ''Let us not move from one extreme
to another, Miss Melville. Undoubtedly there will be
a termination date.''

Which sounded very ominous, Sophie thought. This
prompted her to do something she had not been invited to do. She swept back to her own office, then
headed straight for the filing room to see if there was
a Sullivan dossier. It might not be business that she
needed to know, but it was her solution to the Sullivan wrangle that had got her the job in the first place,
and Sophie had the feeling she was better off if she
stayed six steps ahead of Jason Lombard.

There certainly was a Sullivan file. Scanning quickly
through the papers, she discovered that Jason Lombard had been as thick as thieves with both Gail and
Randy since they had married. He had done all their
legal work for them. She wondered if the close association had sparked the passion that had once existed
between Gail and himself. Was he the figure behind
the scenes, causing or manipulating the drive towards
the divorce court?

''Can I help you, Miss Melville?''

Sophie started guiltily. Jason Lombard was in the
narrow aisle behind her, blocking any exit. ''Merely
doing some homework so I'm prepared for anything,

Mr. Lombard," she answered glibly, doing her best to cover up the fact that he had caught her red-handed.

"I was looking for you. You weren't in your office," he said, moving forward to confirm his suspicions. "I didn't realise you had a passion for prying."

Sophie breathed an exaggerated sigh of resignation. "Another rule. No prying. Even though it might help my boss."

She jammed the file into its slot in the cabinet drawer and was about to slam it shut when a strong hand reached around her and grasped the top edge of the drawer, preventing any closure.

"Not so fast, Miss Melville," he breathed in her ear, and Sophie froze as he leaned past her. "You were looking at the Sullivan file."

"I have a right to know," she pleaded in excuse. "Doesn't my job depend on the successful outcome of this case?"

She whirled around to defend herself more vigorously, inadvertently knocking the drawer, which promptly slid shut, momentarily unbalancing him. He took a step forward, instinctively trying to recover. The result was cataclysmic.

Sophie found herself crushed against him, thigh to thigh, stomach to stomach, her breasts plastered to the hard wall of his chest. She had an instant and overwhelming awareness of ungiving muscularity. She also had an instant and overwhelming desire to stay precisely where she was. Something deeply biological whispered that this was her man and he felt very right to her.

She looked up, instinctively seeking some sign that he felt the same. She had no idea what showed on her face, but her mind was very busily registering the strange thrills running up and down her legs from the powerful pressure of his, and the funny empty feeling in her stomach that yearned for something more than food, and the explosion of sensitivity in her breasts.

There seemed to be some inner conflict warring in his eyes, but the instant they caught her gaze on him, the flickering expressions fused into a clear, focussed intensity that sent a delicious shiver down Sophie's spine. The light in the silvery grey eyes was searingly primitive, arrogantly male, wanting to take, to know, to have. She felt his hands on her hips, the warmth of his palms spreading over the outward curves from her narrow waist. There was an unmistakable stirring in his loins. The tip of his tongue swept over his lips in sensual suggestiveness.

Sophie tilted her head back, inviting the kiss that had to be coming. His gaze dropped to her mouth. It was definitely coming, Sophie thought, breathing in with exultant satisfaction. Her lips parted in anticipation. Her every nerve was aquiver with anticipation as she closed her eyes.

"Mr. Lombard, are you in here?" The crisp question was followed by a shocked, "Oh!"

Sophie's eyes flew open. Her head jerked towards the source of the mood-shattering interruption. Cheryl

Hughes, the receptionist, was standing at the head of the aisle between the filing cabinets, her mouth open in surprise, her eyes agog, her whole face a flood of confusion.

"I, er, I'm sorry to disturb you, sir," Cheryl floundered, then finished in an agitated rush. "But Miss Carstairs has arrived and is demanding to see you."

Without waiting for a reply, she turned on her heel and hastened from the room, decisively closing the door behind her.

The swiftness with which Jason Lombard disengaged himself from Sophie, and the appalled look on his face, immediately incited a need to defend herself.

"You've ruined my reputation," she cried.

"What have you done to mine?" he counteraccused.

The discomfort he was suffering from thwarted desire was all too evident. "I'm going back to my office," she said, and tactfully left him to adjust himself before he had to face the demanding Miss Carstairs.

It was clear to Sophie that while Jason Lombard felt the same physical attraction she did, he was fighting any idea of becoming personally involved with her. Whether this was for professional or private reasons, she did not know. The only absolute certainty was that the time to consolidate her position with him had a termination point that he might be reconsidering right now.

But he couldn't fire her before the Tahiti trip, Sophie assured herself. She was safely entrenched in the job until after that, because he had promised to give her a month's trial. And who knew what might happen in Tahiti, despite Gail Sullivan's presence there?

Sophie did not need to go through the reception area to reach her office, but she was, after all, Jason Lombard's personal assistant, and she saw no reason she shouldn't greet the untimely visitor on his behalf and soothe Miss Carstairs's impatience. Apart from which, Sophie wanted to size up the woman who had caused such a rude interruption to an extremely promising moment.

She was a blonde who oozed sophistication from the top of her silky head to her stylish Italian shoes. She had the tall, slim body that dress designers preferred for showing off their clothes, and Miss Carstairs was showing off a white silk suit that had undoubtedly cost her a mint. She was also showing off less than ladylike manners as she looked Sophie up and down.

"Dear God! What have we here?" she sneered, her eyes scorning the flaming glory of Sophie's hair.

It was too much! Sophie's voice dripped ice as she retorted, "I was about to inquire that of you, Miss Carstairs."

Cheryl Hughes swiftly inserted some saving grace into a potentially explosive moment. "Miss Melville is Mr. Lombard's new personal assistant, Miss Carstairs."

The blonde's eyes widened, then rolled to the receptionist. "You've got to be joking!" Then she looked at Sophie and poured forth a peal of derisive laughter. "Jason hired that as his right hand?" she shrieked. "Has he given her a broomstick yet?"

"Have you had any teeth knocked out lately, Miss Carstairs?" Sophie asked gratingly, her even temper shattering under the pressure of open insults. "Would you like a black eye? Or would you rather have coffee while you're waiting? Milk, sugar or arsenic?"

"That's enough, Miss Melville!" Jason Lombard's voice lashed out. "Evonne, would you please come into my office?"

Sophie whirled on him, her eyes flashing blue dagger points. "Will you be wanting me, as well, Mr. Lombard? Take notes? Act as a witness?"

"Jason, darling, your tie's all awry," the blonde purred, slinking forward to insinuate herself between Sophie and her boss. "Whatever have you been up to?"

He irritably prevented her from straightening his tie and took her arm to steer her forcibly into his office. "Let's get to whatever business brought you here, Evonne," he rasped. His eyes glittered at Sophie. "I won't be needing you any more today, Miss Melville. You may go home early."

"Don't forget your pointy hat," the blonde trilled, and broke into more peals of laughter as Jason Lombard effected her removal from the reception area.

Sophie clenched her hands in seething fury, not only at the blonde's rude mockery, but at Jason Lombard's dismissal of her in favour of his darling Miss Carstairs.

"Don't take any notice of her. She's a bitch."

Cheryl Hughes's sympathetic comment surprised Sophie into spinning around. The receptionist gave her a rueful smile. It was the first friendly gesture Sophie had received from any of the staff.

"You don't think I look like a witch?" Sophie asked with a self-deprecating grimace.

Cheryl's smile stretched into a grin. "I think your hair is fantastic." She touched her own ash-brown conservative style. "I've been wondering all week what it must be like to be so daring. I'd love to change mine to something wild." Her eyes sparkled with a sense of adventure. "If I ever pluck up enough courage to do it, I'll ask you for the name of your hairdresser."

Sophie shook her head in amazement. "I had the impression that everyone here thought I was freakish."

"Just surprised that Mr. Lombard chose you," Cheryl explained. She nodded towards the closed door. "He usually likes to have sleek-looking women around him. She's typical of his taste." Cheryl wrinkled her nose. "Rich bitch! Thinks she can swan it over everybody."

"How long has she been an item in his life?" Sophie asked, hating the thought that Jason Lombard might be seriously attached to such a poisonous woman.

"A few months. Long enough to start thinking she owns him." Her eyes flashed teasingly at Sophie. "But maybe you're teaching him different."

Sophie blushed. "I think we'd both better forget about that, Cheryl. Sheer aberration on his part."

Cheryl rolled her eyes and drew a finger across her throat. "My lips are sealed."

Sophie couldn't help smiling at the explicit gesture. "Me, too," she said, feeling that at least she had one friendly ally. "The hairdressing salon you want is called The Cutting Point. Ask for Mia."

"That's the same place Mr. Lombard's mother recommended to me," Cheryl cried excitedly. "They do super things with her hair, too. She came in last Friday with an apricot base and blonde streaks. It looked great!"

Sophie had the sudden feeling that the earth was shifting under her feet. Her sympathetic listener at the salon fitted that description, but surely her name had been Whitten or something like that. "I don't think I could have met her there," she said. "I would have remembered a Mrs. Lombard."

"It's Mrs. Whitlow. She's been married twice," Cheryl explained offhandedly. "Anyhow, that really makes up my mind. I'm going to call for an appointment and take the plunge."

"Good luck!" Sophie said weakly, her worst suspicions confirmed.

She walked to her office in a daze. The correction letter, granting her an interview, had been sent after she had blurted out all her woes to Jason Lombard's mother. The interview itself took on an entirely new light.

Quite apart from Jason Lombard's shocked reaction to her hair, she had felt he harboured an inbuilt resistance to giving her a chance. The way he had played with his darts indicated a flippant approach to passing the set fifteen minutes with her. Nothing serious. Simply going through the motions until she had challenged him into seriousness.

But she *had* earned a chance at the job, Sophie assured herself with stubborn pride. And she was proving herself capable of it. More than capable. He could not deny that. She would fight to keep this job every inch of the way. By the end of the month he would have to admit she was irreplaceable.

Since she had been granted an early leave, Sophie only had to clear her desk and pick up her handbag, but the moment she entered her office, Evonne Carstairs's voice checked all further movement. Jason Lombard had left open the connecting door between their offices when he had come looking for her earlier.

"What on earth possessed you to choose her, Jason?" the insidiously silky voice lilted. "She'll make a laughing-stock of you with everyone who counts."

Superficial snob, Sophie seethed.

"She's part of my mother's present crusade for the unemployed. I promised to give her a chance," came the dismissive reply.

Sophie fiercely wished he had kept that piece of information to himself, however true it was. It left her open to further put-downs from the catty Miss Carstairs. Who didn't miss the opportunity handed to her.

"Well, that's stretching charity to its outermost limits," the rich bitch mocked. "You can't possibly intend to keep her, darling."

He gave a harsh, self-derisive laugh. "No. I don't intend to keep her beyond the month's trial. She's driving me out of my mind as it is."

Something tight and painful clamped around Sophie's heart.

"Then why hold on that long?"

"Because she serves a purpose for which she is perfect."

"Business?"

"What else? I want her as a distraction in a little scheme I have in hand. So keep your claws off, Evonne. I'm not amused by interference in my business."

The cold, calculating bastard! He deserved a nasty bitch like Evonne Carstairs! They deserved each other!

In grim fury, Sophie stalked over to her desk, snatched up her handbag, then marched straight into Jason Lombard's office to confront her two detractors.

It was a cosy little scene with Jason Lombard half inclined in his swinging leather chair and Evonne Carstairs propped on the desk beside him, playfully running her fingernails over his hand. Sophie's entrance startled them out of their self-satisfied contemplation of each other.

"You should close doors before discussing another person behind her back, Mr. Lombard," Sophie fired at him, then swept a blazing look of contempt over both of them. "The way you and Miss Carstairs were talking about me goes beyond the pale of good manners. It shows a callous lack of consideration for the feelings of another human being."

She gave them no time for a reply. Her gaze fastened bitterly on the man who had seemed so right for her. "I'll be out of your hair now, Mr. Lombard. Out of your mind. Out of your life. And out of your schemes."

She tossed her head high, and with all the defiant dignity of a queen scorning unworthy criticism, she crossed the room to the door that opened into the reception area.

"What a scheming little minx!" Evonne Carstairs shot at Sophie's back. "She must have opened the door herself to eavesdrop."

"Miss Melville!"

Sophie ignored the commanding crack of Jason Lombard's voice, ignored the clatter of movement that suggested he'd sprung up from his chair. Her hand closed around the doorknob, turned it, pulled.

"Miss Melville—Sophie, please wait!"

"Oh, for God's sake, Jason! Let her go! Good riddance!"

It was the jeer in Evonne Carstairs's voice that goaded Sophie into swinging around in the doorway. Her eyes shot a last bolt of blue lightning at Jason Lombard, who had belittled her to such a mean woman. How dared he condescend to call her Sophie now!

"Too late, Mr. Lombard," she hurled at him. "You preached discretion and have just practised the nastiest of all indiscretions. You insisted on a vow of silence, but let your own tongue loose with a woman so ill-bred that your judgement is contemptible. Anyone who thinks the colour and style of a woman's hair are more important than her character is far too blind and shallow to be worth working for. I gave you all you demanded in a personal assistant. And you cannot even treat me with respect."

Tears pricked at her eyes. She felt a drop form and start trickling down her right cheek. She swung away, mortified at showing any sign of distress. She stepped out into the reception room, driven now to put this place and everyone in it behind her.

Cheryl Hughes was on her feet behind the reception desk, her attention galvanised by the scene she was witnessing. Other staff members had trailed into the corridor, drawn by the raised voices. Sophie's exit from the reception area was blocked by a middle-aged woman with apricot hair who clapped her hands in admiration.

"Oh, well said! What a splendidly spirited girl!"

"Miss Melville!" Jason Lombard thundered from his doorway.

"Jason! Forget the stupid little upstart," Evonne Carstairs cried in exasperation.

"Shut up, Evonne!"

"Really, Jason!"

"Oh, go to hell! Sophie..."

"I think he wants to apologise, dear," Sophie's admirer said, urging a pause for redress to be made.

"It's too late," Sophie choked out, shaking her head at the sympathetic lady who had brought her into all this in the first place.

Then Jason Lombard was beside her, making his own appeal for forbearance. "We need to talk this out," he said gravely.

"There's nothing more to say," Sophie insisted, her voice wobbling with the weight of a thousand disappointed hopes.

"I think there is."

"No." She forced herself to look up at him one last time, the pain he had given her and pride in her own worth mixing through a luminous film of tears. "I admired you... I respected you—" no need to tell him she had been close to falling in love with him "—and all you saw in me was someone to use...meanly, Mr. Lombard."

"I'm sorry."

"It hurts."

"I truly am sorry."

Sophie shook her head. Impossible to accept that as genuine after what she'd heard him say. "You set out to hurt me with deliberate premeditation."

"I thought I was doing you a favour."

"You weren't. Goodbye, Mr. Lombard."

She walked away from him, and kept on walking this time. An elevator was providentially waiting at the top floor. It zoomed her down to the world of the unemployed.

She told herself she didn't care. She didn't care about the flood of tears that kept choking her, either. She had a right to cry if she wanted to. The unemployed were free to weep. Any time they liked.

CHAPTER FIVE

SOPHIE WALKED AND WALKED, mindless of where she was going or what she passed by. She felt as though something of immeasurable value had been torn away from her, leaving in its wake an irrecoverable sense of loss and desolation.

A dream, she told herself, a stupid, self-deluding dream. She should probably be grateful to Evonne Carstairs for bringing her crashing down to earth. Yet the thought of that woman, on terms of intimate understanding with Jason Lombard, only seemed to make the hurt worse. He should have known better.

It was not until the rush-hour crowds pressed Sophie into a realisation that the working day was at an end that she remembered where she was supposed to be this evening. By then it was too late to telephone Mia at the salon and call off the arrangement they had made.

She found herself closer to the railway station at Milson's Point than North Sydney, but it only made a few minutes' difference in travelling time to Lindfield. With a sense of dull resignation, Sophie caught a train and spent the next twenty minutes trying to work out how to tell her friend what had happened.

The plain truth was that Sophie didn't want to dredge through the whole painful business again, with Mia asking endless questions. She didn't want to talk about it. Not tonight. Perhaps tomorrow, when she felt less raw.

She alighted from the train at Lindfield and trudged up the steps to the pedestrian overpass that led to the shopping centre. So many times she and Mia had passed by Pommeroys Restaurant on their way home to their flat or on the way to some takeaway establishment for a cheap meal. They had promised themselves they would definitely go there when a special occasion warranted the expense. It now seemed bitterly ironic that tonight of all nights had been decided upon, a special treat to mark the end of her first week in her splendid new job.

She spotted Mia already waiting for her on the sidewalk outside the entrance to the restaurant. Sophie did her best to adopt a bright demeanour so her friend would not suspect there was anything wrong. She did not want to spoil Mia's enjoyment of something she had been fancying for months.

The moment Mia saw Sophie, her face lit with delighted anticipation and she rushed forward to link her arm with Sophie's in happy companionship. "At last!" she cried. "I was about to call your boss and demand that he unchain you from your desk. I've so much to tell you. And I'm dying of hunger, as well."

"Sorry I'm late, Mia. I honestly didn't notice the time passing," Sophie said.

She didn't need to say anything else. Mia was only too eager to sweep her into the restaurant and get the business of being settled at a table over so that she could freely burst into triumphant glee.

"You've made me famous, Sophie!" she declared. "Or, at least, I made you famous, so that it rebounded back on me. You wouldn't believe how many calls we had at the salon this afternoon, all wanting to make an appointment with Mia." She preened. "No-one else would do. It had to be me."

Sophie didn't see the connection between herself and Mia's sudden rise in favour with clients.

"It must have been winning the competition," Mia burbled on. "They all want to have their hair coloured and styled just like yours."

"Like mine?" Sophie repeated in surprise.

"Absolutely. I'm going to be raced off my feet tomorrow. Busy, busy, busy. Ten perms, ten cuts, ten colours. I'll have a production line going. Isn't that fantastic?"

"Ten women want hair like mine?" Sophie asked incredulously.

Mia laughed. "I can hardly believe it myself, but it's true, Sophie. It was bedlam trying to fit the appointments in. They came in a rush, one after the other, and it had to be tomorrow. No other day would do for them."

"Maybe it's some mad practical joke," Sophie said, hoping Mia's glorious bubble of fame was not going to be deflated.

"No way. They were passionately set on having me give them what I've given you. Even if they had to pay me extra for working past my normal hours."

Sophie shook her head in bemusement. "Well, it's certainly great business for you, Mia. Congratulations!"

She grinned. "It wouldn't have happened without having you as my advertisement, Sophie. Though I might have to talk them into some other colour and style once I have them in my grasp. Depends on their skin tone and the shape of their faces. I doubt all ten of them will have your pale creamy skin and a face with great bones that can get away with anything. I hope they have the good sense to accept my professional expertise."

"I'm sure they'll listen to you, Mia," Sophie said dryly. With her rapid-fire delivery and a captive audience, Mia could probably mesmerise her clients into accepting anything she advised.

A waiter presented them with menus, and Mia's attention was instantly diverted to food. The merits of every dish had to be discussed before the final choice was made for their dinner. Mia had an appetite that Sophie didn't have a hope of matching tonight, but the easiest course of action was to pretend interest in the cheapest and plainest items on the menu.

Once their order was taken, Mia leaned forward, her bright brown eyes sparkling with the pleasure of knowing something that she considered particularly titillating. "I bet I can tell you something about the

Sullivan affair that you and your boss might like to know.''

Sophie raised her eyebrows inquiringly. While there was no longer any advantage to her in knowing anything more about the Sullivans, trying to discourage Mia from telling a story she was intent on telling was a totally futile exercise.

''Randy Sullivan is dropping out,'' she declared excitedly. ''And you'll never guess where he's going.''

Sophie tensed, wondering what information had been leaked and by whom. Then she bitterly reminded herself that it was no longer of any concern to her.

''You know how we reckoned that he and Gail should be dumped on a deserted island together to sort out their differences?'' Mia paused for appropriate encouragement. `

''Yes,'' Sophie obliged.

''Well, he's flying off to one. His travel agent was getting her hair done today, and she said he's booked a trip to Bora Bora.''

If that became public knowledge, Jason Lombard was certain to think she had leaked it, Sophie thought, mentally piling one more injustice onto her heap of grievances against him. Yet it gave her no sense of satisfaction that his scheme for the Sullivans might come unstuck. She had wanted to help make it right again between them.

"It's a pity someone couldn't organise for Gail to go there, too," Mia went on. "Who could keep quarrelling in a tropical paradise?"

"I suppose it depends on how blind they've become to what's real and what isn't," Sophie remarked flatly. "There's none so blind as those who don't want to see."

Like Jason Lombard, who refused to look past her hair! To plan on using her as a distraction was a demeaning insult to her capabilities. She could have really helped him if he'd given her the chance. A woman's point of view might have made an enormous difference in dealing with the warring couple.

Having been involved in the problem all week, Sophie found herself wishing that the scheme could work. She leaned forward and impulsively appealed to her friend. "Mia, could you stop everyone at the salon from spreading that piece of news about Randy Sullivan?"

Mia looked shocked. "No way! That would amount to censorship. We can't have that. It's an unwritten rule of our profession. The news must go through. Our clients wouldn't trust us to tell them everything if we started holding back."

"I simply thought that if Gail heard about Randy's trip, wild horses wouldn't drag her to Bora Bora," Sophie explained.

Her friend's bright brown eyes widened, her agile mind instantly putting two and two together. "Is Gail likely to be going there? Is this what you've been working on with Jason Lombard?''

Sophie sighed. ''I can't tell you that, Mia.''

Although her sense of integrity insisted on clinging to the rule of confidentiality, Sophie hated the feeling of deceiving Mia about her position. If the waiter had not fortuitously arrived to serve them with their starters, she would have blurted out the truth. However, one look at the food placed in front of her was reminder enough that it wouldn't be fair to rob Mia of her pleasure in eating.

Sophie managed to do some justice to the smoked salmon cornet while Mia ploughed through her crepe with crispy duck topped with spicy mango sauce. However, when they were presented with their main courses, her stomach went into rebellion. She pushed the John Dory fillets around the plate while Mia hoed into her rich concoction of veal steak with lobster medallions and prawns in a light brandy sauce, topped with macadamia nuts. Mia applied the same zest to eating as she did to talking, and her plate was polished clean of everything before Sophie had made any start at all.

''Something wrong with what you ordered?'' she asked in belated concern, then was promptly distracted into looking straight past Sophie. ''Wow!'' she breathed. ''Don't look now, but a ten on the male Richter scale just walked in!''

The outstanding classification made no impression on Sophie. She couldn't be less interested in men at the moment. She flaked off a small piece of fish with her fork, wondering if she could slide it down her throat.

"I've caught his eye," Mia hissed in excitement. "He's by himself and he's heading straight towards me."

And will undoubtedly walk right past, Sophie thought.

But he didn't.

Mia's uninhibited come-hither look had apparently hit some ready chord of response. The man stopped at their table. Sophie kept her eyes fixed on her dinner plate, disassociating herself from any social entanglement with the situation. She prodded at a piece of potato with total disinterest. It was up to Mia to handle whatever she wanted to invite.

"Can I help you?" Mia asked brightly, radiating a welcoming warmth and interest.

"I hope so," came the unmistakable voice of Jason Lombard.

Sophie's head jerked up. The fork she had been holding dropped from suddenly nerveless fingers and clattered onto the plate. Her whole body stiffened in violent rejection as her eyes met the intensity of purpose gleaming from his.

"Wow!" Mia breathed, hit by the electricity of two opposing elements.

"What are you doing here?" Sophie accused, more than asked. "Haven't you already spoilt enough for me?"

He winced, but the silver-grey eyes held hers unwaveringly. "I went to your flat. You weren't there. I had to find you. I thought I might meet you coming off a train so I walked this way and happened to glance into the restaurant . . ."

"And saw my bright, distracting hair," Sophie cut in with bitter sarcasm.

"I would have waited all night to speak to you, if need be. To tell you how sorry I am for what happened—"

"You've already said that," Sophie snapped, disturbed and confused by his persistence. "Consider your apology accepted, Mr. Lombard," she added with cold finality.

"Lombard?" Mia echoed incredulously. "Your boss?"

"Not any more," Sophie bit out.

"Please hear me out," he asked, refusing to be dismissed.

"Why?"

"Because I admire you," he said softly. "Because I respect you. Because I was terribly, terribly wrong. Because saying I'm sorry is not the end but the beginning of making amends."

"Oh!" sighed Mia, reduced to mush by the seductive flow of appeasement.

Sophie stubbornly kept her heart rock-hard. Words were the tools of an advocate's trade. Of course, Jason Lombard could use them to sway his listeners when he knew who his listeners were. It was his bad luck he had slipped up this afternoon and revealed his true form. Sophie was not about to forget that in a hurry, no matter what he said now.

She regarded him with relentlessly unforgiving eyes. "There's nothing you can do—"

"Please let me try."

Mia suddenly hopped up from the table, all sweetness and light as she seized the role of peacemaker. "You can have my chair, Mr. Lombard. I've finished my dinner, and I really must dash. There's a call I simply have to make. You'll see Sophie home safely, won't you?"

Before he could reply, Mia had skipped around him to hold Sophie in her chair under the pretence of a friendly hug. "To err is human, to forgive is divine," she crooned, then lowered her voice to whisper into Sophie's ear. "You're mad if you let him get away! Grab him!"

Then she was off in a whirl, airily waving away all responsibility for what she left behind, including payment for the meal she had eaten. Sophie half-rose from her chair in protest, only to sink back in helpless resignation when all there was to confront was the door closing behind Mia's swift exit.

She glared up at Jason Lombard, who had not yet availed himself of the chair Mia had offered him. "You might have fooled my friend, Mr. Lombard," she said in fierce resentment. "But don't think I can be fooled into taking anything you say at face value."

His mouth tilted into an ironic little smile. "There is only one fool here, Miss Melville. And that is myself. You were absolutely right this afternoon. My judgement, especially where you are concerned, has been appalling."

This surprising admission did not anaesthetise the hurt he had given her, but it went some way towards soothing the humiliation of having been taken in by his deceit. She eyed him warily, unsure that he wasn't setting out to deceive her again. There had to be some reason behind his chasing after her. She couldn't believe he cared that much about recovering her good opinion of him.

"May I sit down?" he asked, gesturing towards the chair Mia had vacated for him.

"By all means," she answered, mocking his projection of sincerity as she added, "if you really think it's worth your time."

"Thank you," he said, giving her an apologetic smile as he sat opposite her. "I didn't mean to spoil your dinner. That food must be cold by now. Can I order something else for you?"

"I'm not hungry," Sophie stated flatly.

"Coffee?"

"If you like."

He signalled a waiter. Jason Lombard was one of those people who automatically commanded good service. He had that air of class and authority that expected the best from others and invariably received it. The table was swiftly cleared. Coffee was promptly served. A plate of after-dinner mints accompanied the coffee.

Sophie watched it all happen with cynical eyes. Mia was right, she thought. Jason Lombard was a ten on the male Richter scale in every superficial sense. She doubted there was a woman alive who wouldn't find him attractive, who wouldn't enjoy having him pay attention to her. But Sophie clamped down severely on the treacherous female vulnerability he stirred in her. All this caring attention had to be a sham.

The moment they were left alone, she fired a direct challenge at him. "Let's get straight to the point, Mr. Lombard. You haven't come after me to grovel for forgiveness or do a repair job on your image. I'm too unimportant in your life to bother about that. So what's your purpose?"

CHAPTER SIX

SOPHIE WAS SATISFIED that she had pulled the mat out from under Jason Lombard's feet and left him floundering with the choice of delivering bare honesty or being swept out the door.

Clearly the choice was not to his liking. For several long moments he sought a way around it, weighing his chances of succeeding. The knowing derision in Sophie's eyes apparently convinced him there was no point in wavering.

"I want you to come to Bora Bora with me," he said.

Sophie could hardly believe her ears. "You expect me to accept such a proposal after what you said about me this afternoon?"

He leaned forward, appealing to her with urgent intensity. "I want your forgiveness, but I intend to earn it, not talk about it, beg or grovel for it. I'm offering you an opportunity to have your job back, to take a new look at your future and reassess what may be possible between us."

Sophie raised mocking eyebrows. "Another trial, Mr. Lombard? Which will last until I've served the purpose you had in mind for me?"

"Forget what I said this afternoon!" he pressed earnestly. "This is different!"

Forgetting was too tall an order for Sophie. "Why not ask Miss Carstairs to fill in for me? I'm sure she'd be only too happy to provide the little distraction you require for your Bora Bora scheme."

He winced. "Evonne Carstairs and I parted company this afternoon. I have no desire whatsoever to resurrect any personal involvement with her."

"Poor judgement in the first place," Sophie sniped, nevertheless feeling a fine satisfaction in the rich bitch's fall from favour.

"It was a mutual social convenience," Jason Lombard muttered, impatiently dismissing the contentious relationship.

"You couldn't find someone better than her?" Sophie jabbed at him, fiercely resenting his betrayal of her to such a woman.

Irritation tightened his face. "I wasn't particularly looking."

"I take it she fitted your purpose well enough." Sophie's eyes glittered scorn. "I presume she made up for her shortcomings in character with her performance in bed. Did you enjoy her catty claws there, Mr. Lombard?"

Frustration glittered in his eyes. "Can we move past Evonne Carstairs? As I recall, you gave back as good as you got from her this afternoon, and the honours went to you. I told you she's gone."

"Why is she gone? You put me down in a quite un-conscionable manner in order to keep her sweet—"

"I told you I'm sorry for doing that. And I am," he said with considerable vehemence.

"So you broke off with her in some fit of remorse over hurting me?"

"No. I should never have had any concern about her opinion of me." He grimaced, then glowered at Sophie, his eyes burning with a heat that sizzled with male sexuality. "I have no excuse for not defending you. In effect, you made me realise that I didn't want Evonne Carstairs in my life any more. Not for any-thing."

"Well, that's a step in the right direction," Sophie drawled, feeling a very primitive wave of exultation over this admission. Maybe Cheryl Hughes was right, and she *was* teaching him a different appreciation of women. Sophie liked his phrase about the honours going to her this afternoon.

She remembered the accidental step he had taken in the filing room, the desire for her that had swept everything else from his mind. She suddenly had the feeling that he was remembering it, too, and her heart skittered nervously as she wondered if he wanted to explore that kind of possibility between them in the future he was offering her.

She sipped her coffee, giving herself time to consider all Jason Lombard had said so far. Maybe he still wanted to use her for his own ends, then get rid of her at his convenience, but he had apologised very handsomely, and made some considerable amends by finally having the good judgement to prefer her to Evonne Carstairs.

Besides, there was nothing attractive about being unemployed, and there was quite a bit to be said for a free trip to Tahiti.

"Sophie..." He gave her name a husky softness that sent a delicious thrill down her spine. He frowned as though he had surprised himself with it, then hastily added, "We need to be on first-name terms. Please call me Jason."

"I haven't agreed to anything," she reminded him, but her objections to a reassessment of the future had been substantially eroded.

He made an earnest gesture with his hands, and Sophie thought she detected real caring in his eyes as he said, "What more can I say?"

"It's a matter of attitude towards me," she explained. "Firstly, I find the idea of being used as a little distraction personally demeaning. Secondly, if you keep your scheme for the Sullivan reconciliation to yourself, you're going to stuff it up."

"Why do you say that?" he demanded, affronted by the slight on his capabilities.

"You're personally involved in the outcome. You must know as well as I do that any attorney who advocates his own cause can't be objective. You're bound to stuff it up. You need an independent adviser to keep you out of trouble."

His eyes hardened. "Miss Melville," he bit out in a tone of exasperation, the soft appeasement of *Sophie* tossed aside in favour of laying down the line of authority. Then he checked himself and reorganised his demeanour to one of amenable reasoning. "I shall listen to whatever advice you wish to give me. But *I* make the decisions."

To Sophie's mind, an assistant should be in on the decisions, and if Jason Lombard really did respect and admire her, he owed her a few more concessions. "How long do you reckon it will take for this scheme of yours to work?" she asked.

"Three days. Maybe four," he answered confidently.

"You booked accommodation for seven days."

"Some rest and relaxation will undoubtedly be in order after we've tied everything back together again. Do you have some objection to that?"

"None at all. If there's time." She smiled. "I'll make a deal with you."

"What do you have in mind?" he asked warily.

"You can make the decisions for the first four days. If your scheme hasn't worked by then, you give me a free hand with the decision-making for the rest of our week there."

He sucked in a long breath and heaved a very deep sigh. His eyes glittered a rueful appreciation of her bargaining ability. "You are a damned hard woman, Miss Melville!"

"And you are a damned hard man, Mr. Lombard!" she retorted.

"It's a deal," he conceded. "Call me Jason."

She gave him her brightest smile this time. "Then we're back to Sophie."

He stared at her mouth for several seconds, emanating the kind of feeling that suggested to Sophie that he would like very much to ravish it into submission. A little tingle of excitement spread through her veins. She never had liked weak men. On the other hand, she didn't fancy being dominated, either. What she wanted with Jason Lombard was a real sense of partnership.

He recollected himself and got back to business. "Are you prepared to fly out with me next Friday? I've organised Randy—"

"Too late," she said. "The news is already out. If you don't have both Gail and Randy in Bora Bora by Monday, the whole scheme will be blown."

"How could the news get out?" he demanded, appalled at the possibility that his plans might be wrecked before he could put them into effect. "I only told my mother this afternoon, and she promised not to say a word."

"Randy Sullivan's travel agent had her hair done today."

"Oh, my God!"

"You can count on half of Sydney knowing it by tomorrow."

"That fast?"

"Every woman knows you get the real news at the hairdressers'."

He groaned. "What the hell do we do now?"

"Reorganise the arrangements," she advised. "And use what influence you have to keep Gail secluded until we can all fly out."

He sipped his coffee while he cogitated over Sophie's advice, apparently seeing its good sense and accepting the necessity of plotting a new course. Sophie waited patiently, pleased with the way things were developing between them. She reflected that he hadn't once stared at her hair, which surely meant he accepted it as part and parcel of the person she was. Which was another step in the right direction!

"Right!" he said, putting his cup down with firm precision. His silver-grey eyes gleamed with satisfaction. "I can keep everything stable for a few days. We fly out Monday evening."

"Great!" Sophie approved.

"Finished your coffee?"

"Ready to leave," she affirmed.

He signalled the waiter for the bill, took out his wallet from an inner coat pocket, and also a thick envelope, which he handed across to Sophie.

"What's in this?" she asked suspiciously.

"Wages for the week. Agony money. Clothing expenses for the trip."

Her blue eyes widened in astonishment. "How do you measure agony?"

"It's a trick we lawyers have," he said dryly. "We inevitably end up measuring everything in money terms."

Sophie buttoned down her sense of outrage. It was clear to her that Jason Lombard needed to have his thinking retrained, and she was just the person to do it. After all, she had obviously made a strong impression on his thinking this afternoon and had already made several inroads on it tonight, as well. With more opportunities to whip him into shape, he might very well turn out to be the right man for her.

In the meantime, she was curious to know the amount of compensation he thought she deserved for the hurt he had given her.

"I'll count it carefully when I get home," she said. "And see how far you're out."

"Let me know the shortfall."

"Oh, I certainly will," said Sophie. "I'll give you my best advice on it."

He caught the mocking note in her voice and flashed her a wary look that gave Sophie the impression he found her uncomfortably unpredictable. Maybe it was that element about her that drove him out of his mind. Or it could be the physical chemistry, Sophie reasoned. Whatever it was, she had certainly shaken him up. Which was all to the good.

He seemed to greet the arrival of the bill with relief. He threw down some notes and rose abruptly to his feet.

"I should pay..." Sophie began to protest.

He made a dismissive gesture, and the proudly determined look on his face brooked no opposition. Jason Lombard was set on recovering his position as master of the situation, and Sophie decided this was not an issue worth fighting over. With a sigh of resignation she rose from the table.

"May I see you home?" he asked with gentlemanly courtesy.

"Well, if your car is parked outside our apartment block, there's not much point in our going separate ways," she said, her own pride insisting she not appear too submissive to his will.

As they made their exit from the restaurant, an important thought occurred to Sophie. She knew how much her wage should be, but how was she going to separate the agony money from the clothes money? She was contemplating how to pose this delicate question when she felt a strong male hand wrap itself warmly and firmly around hers.

She slid a sideways glance at the man beside her, wondering what he meant by it. He was looking down the street, apparently wrapped in his own thoughts and unaware that he had done anything untoward. Then his fingers started playing over hers in a slow experimental caress, as though he would like to get under her skin.

Which was precisely what was happening.

The contact was stirring a range of physical responses that were very distracting to Sophie's train of thought. She barely stopped her own fingers from exploring the feel of his.

What did he think he was doing? Holding hands didn't fit into her idea of a straight employer-employee relationship. Not that she wanted one, but this move from him was definitely suspect, coming on top of everything else. Having gained her acceptance to his proposition, did he now think he could do anything he liked with her? Whenever he liked?

"Why are you holding my hand?" she blurted out.

He gave her a surprised look. "I'm protecting you from tripping in the dark."

"Oh!" said Sophie. It was a few more moments before she observed that the street was quite well lit. She threw his profile another surreptitious glance and saw that his lips wore a slight upward curve that smacked of self-satisfaction.

"I wouldn't want you to forget about male problems," she fired at him.

"Believe me, Sophie, they are at the forefront of my mind," he smoothly assured her.

Sophie found this remark highly disturbing. Snatching her hand away from his seemed overly prissy. Better to ignore it, she decided, and try to switch both their minds onto something else.

Which brought her back to the thick envelope he had given her. "What figure did you arrive at for covering my clothing expenses for the trip?" she asked.

"My mother worked that out, so it should be about right," he said.

"Well, what did she decide?"

He sighed. "Since you've only recently changed your hair from brown to, uh, that rather unique shade of red, you obviously need an entirely new wardrobe for this trip so you can create the right impression. My mother figured three thousand dollars should cover everything, so that's what I put in the envelope."

"Three..." Sophie swallowed hard and bit her lips. Who was she to question a woman who was promoting her cause? From the pained patience in Jason Lombard's voice, apparently Mrs. Whitlow, who had so admired Sophie's stand this afternoon, had given her son quite a haranguing stream of advice.

"What impression am I supposed to create?" she asked. "Am I supposed to be demure, or quietly sophisticated, or—"

"With your hair?" he said incredulously. "No way! My mother's right. You go for a totally dazzling image. Since you already stand out from the crowd, you take it all the way with your clothes. But nothing cheap. Classy flamboyant was the way my mother put it. Make it a very stylish affair."

Sophie was liking Jason's mother more by the minute. "What kind of clothes do you think would be suitably stylish?"

"I forgot to bring the list. As I recall, it had two bikinis, some mix and match shorts and tops, a few classy casual numbers for dinner and a couple of those sarong things. But you can change that to whatever you like."

"I take it that this image is to impress the Sullivans?"

"Yes."

"A distraction."

"Yes." Then he hastily added, "Though, of course, I will listen to your advice, Sophie."

"Where does your mother usually shop, Jason?" Sophie asked curiously.

"Oh, everywhere," he answered vaguely. "Though, come to mention it, she did say to tell you Double Bay had a good range of those things. Might save you some time looking around. You'll only have tomorrow to shop."

That accounted for the three thousand, Sophie thought. Double Bay was one of the most exclusive shopping centres in Sydney, chock-a-block with designer wear.

Sophie noticed a top-of-the-line BMW parked at the kerb in front of her apartment block. "Your car?"

"Yes."

"Well, I'm perfectly safe from here," Sophie, said, starting to disengage her hand.

His grip tightened. "I'll see you to your door. Your friend asked me to."

Somehow Sophie felt much more conscious of him beside her once they were inside the building. He did not release her hand until they were on the landing outside the first-floor flat she and Mia occupied. Then she was all thumbs as she fumbled in her handbag for her key. He waited patiently, not moving away. It was quite a relief to find the key and shove it into the lock.

She turned towards him, feeling hopelessly fluttery inside. He searched her eyes intently for a few nerve-tingling moments, then his mouth curved into a smile that was so full of male confidence and satisfaction that Sophie wondered if she had revealed how vulnerable she was to his physical appeal.

"I'll come by for you on Monday morning," he said. "Eight-thirty."

"You don't need to do that," Sophie protested in a somewhat breathless voice.

"You'll have luggage with you. Besides, I want to make sure you don't change your mind."

He had thought about kissing her. Sophie was sure of it. The fact that he had decided to play safe for the sake of keeping her on line for the job ahead of them in no way diminished the desire, which could wait for a more propitious time and place.

"I'll be ready," she assured him. Ready to take appropriate action if he came on to her too fast at Bora Bora, she sternly advised herself. She opened the door, stepped inside the flat, then gave him a cheeky grin before closing the door on him. "Good night, Jason. Better go home and consult the omens."

CHAPTER SEVEN

MIA POUNCED the moment she saw that Sophie had come in alone. "What was he guilty of?" was the first question off the firing line.

Sophie deflected it. "I'll be going away next week, Mia. Leaving Monday."

Mia's mind revolved with lightning speed and shot out, "Do you think you'll solve the Sullivan wrangle?"

"I've got a lot to do tomorrow, so I think I'll have an early night," Sophie said, knowing how tricky Mia could be at winkling out information.

"Did he pay for our dinner?"

That was fairly safe ground. "Yes, he did."

Mia looked smug. "Well, if I were you, Sophie, I'd play for keeps next week. That guy is loaded with everything."

"That remains to be seen."

It was another half hour before Mia gave up speculating on what she had seen of Jason Lombard and what she would do if he were her boss. Luckily tomorrow was going to be a busy day for her, as well, so when Sophie again pressed for an early night, Mia was agreeable.

As soon as her friend was settled for sleep and Sophie was assured of privacy in her bedroom, she slit open the thick envelope and counted thirty hundred-dollar notes. That was the money for clothes. Then she put aside her wages. The rest had to be the agony money.

She started counting again.

There were another thirty hundred-dollar notes.

Mrs. Whitlow, Sophie decided, was having a very beneficial affect on her son. Or agony was a very lucrative business to be in. Or Jason Lombard was determined on wiping the slate clean with a sweetener so large he'd win more than forgiveness.

Was he looking to press some advantage with her in giving so much? Was he in the habit of thinking that women could be bought? Did he work on the principle that if you put enough sugar on the pill, anything could be swallowed?

Sophie stacked the notes into the envelope and slid it under her pillow. She turned off the light and settled herself for sleep, thinking she had never had such an up and down day in her whole life. After reviewing all that had happened, she came to one firm decision. The agony money would go in the bank for a rainy day. If Jason Lombard proved to be an unredeemable rat, it would certainly ease her agony to throw his thirty hundred-dollar notes back at him in a rain of contempt.

She hoped it wouldn't turn out that way. She desperately wanted her instincts to be right. It was the

feeling of having been hopelessly deceived by them
that had so deeply distressed her this afternoon.

Sophie lay in the darkness wondering about the
"rightness" she felt with Jason Lombard. While she
couldn't precisely define it, she knew she had never
experienced it before. She had found plenty of other
men attractive, several times playing with the idea that
one or other of them might be right for her, but that
had been more a mental measuring of their suitability
or compatibility, never an instinctive thing.

Biology and chemistry were very tricky, Sophie decided. But at least she had a job again. Whatever else
happened with Jason Lombard would require careful
judgement. Despite all her logical reasoning there was
still some instinct inside her urging her to do precisely
what Mia advised: go all out to grab the man for
keeps!

That totally primitive motivation was highly oper-
ative in many of Sophie's choices the next day. Freed
of any constraint to be the least bit conservative, she
had a wonderful shopping spree. To be uninhibitedly
flamboyant, she found, gave one a deliciously spicy
feeling. If a dazzling distraction was what Jason
Lombard wanted, he was certainly going to get it. He
couldn't argue that Sophie had not followed orders.

Mia took charge of all activities on Sunday. Having
drooled over the clothes Sophie had bought, she insisted that they experiment with complementary make-
up and nail polish for an absolutely overall stylish image. She dug out some beautician products she had

stored away, gave Sophie a facial, shampooed and blow-dried her hair into perfect shape and generally acted as though she were preparing Sophie to become Jason Lombard's concubine.

"This is a business trip," Sophie reminded her more than once, although not too strongly since they were both enjoying the fun.

"It never hurts to optimise one's chances," was Mia's unbudgeable stance.

Even on Monday morning Mia was like a maid on harem duty, supervising Sophie's toilet before leaving for work, then flashing a V-for-victory sign to her from the door.

When Jason arrived at eight-thirty, Sophie was more than ready to get on with the job she had been grooming herself for, both outwardly and inwardly, since he had left her on Friday night. The first thing she noticed when she opened the door to him was his business suit, which threw her into a fluster.

"Oh! I dressed for travel. Do you want me to change into something more decorous for the office?"

He looked her up and down. Very slowly. The dress she had chosen to wear was definitely eye-catching. Splashes of bright yellow, fire red, electric blue and jewel green formed a vaguely floral pattern on a white background. Roulade bands of gold and blue and green made feature finishes around the armholes, the scooped neckline and the hemline, emphasising the belt made of the same featured bands. The soft cotton fabric had some silky mixture in it that made it uncrushable, and the slim-line form-fitting cut of the dress made the most of Sophie's curves. Spectacular and stylish, Sophie had thought, especially with the yellow sandals and carry bag.

She watched Jason's expression anxiously, willing him to be pleased with her choice. There was a slightly dazed look in his eyes when his gaze finally returned to hers. He took a deep breath, apparently to gather himself, then gave her a smile that tingled right down to Sophie's toes.

"Couldn't be more perfect," he declared with satisfaction.

His approval was so sweet that Sophie glowed right back at him with a dazzling smile of her own.

He abruptly leaned forward and snatched up her luggage. His face was set with determined purpose as he stepped back to give her room to move past him. "Let's get going," he said briskly. "There's a lot to get through today since the schedule on this has been moved forward."

Sophie quickly stepped out of the flat and checked that the door had locked behind her. "How did it go with Gail Sullivan?" she tossed over her shoulder as she preceded him down the stairs.

"She flew out last night. She'd be on the island by now."

"And Randy Sullivan?"

"I persuaded him into bringing his trip forward. He'll get there Wednesday instead of Friday."

"Does that suit you?"

"It will have to. It was the only way I could work it, and that took some doing."

"Want to tell me about it?" Sophie invited hopefully.

"Later. Too much else to think of right now."

It was strictly business all the way to the office. Sophie had the impression he was deliberately shutting off any personal element between them. Which was only sensible, she reasoned, during work hours. She was sure it would be different once they were free of office responsibilities. She ran her fingers reassuringly over the skirt of her perfect dress and listened hard to everything he said.

Jason listed the various appointments that would need postponing, the pending legal problems that would have to be passed on to his associates to deal with, important matters he had to handle himself before flying out tonight. They had a very full day ahead of them.

Sophie's mind was so occupied with working out how she could best assist him, she completely forgot her return to the office might cause some surprise amongst the staff after the somewhat public showdown with Jason and Evonne Carstairs last Friday. She was totally unprepared for what they met in the reception area.

All the women on the staff were gathered around Cheryl Hughes's desk. There were several moments of frozen shock while they gaped at Sophie, who was very conspicuously at Jason Lombard's side. The shock was mutual. She and Jason were confronted by ten heads of red hair, all in varying shades and styles, but uniformly and uncompromisingly red, shouting a bold and rebellious statement without saying a word.

Mia's production line, Sophie thought in speechless amazement.

"Very becoming," Jason said, surprising them all with his ready acceptance. "It gives our establishment a style we've never had before. And a sense of solidarity that I keenly appreciate."

He paused, bestowing a smile around the group. "However, since Miss Melville and I will be flying out to Bora Bora tonight, there's no time to waste today. May I suggest we all get to work, ladies?"

There was a visible jerk to attention and a flurry of respectful agreement as they quickly dispersed to their workplaces. Jason took Sophie's arm and swept her into his office, very much the man in command.

It was a hectic day. Having defused the feminist uprising, Jason apparently dismissed it from his mind, and Sophie didn't dare question him about what he really thought. Although she admired the way he had handled the situation, she suspected that such openly mutinous criticism of how he had dealt with her could not be very palatable. Nevertheless, it gave her a warm glow inside to know that all the women on the staff were solidly behind her rejection of shabby treatment.

"It was for ourselves, as well," Cheryl explained when they managed a few moments' chat. "We're sick of falling in with men's expectations. They can respect us as people in our own right for a change. Besides—" she grinned "—we've all had a ball this weekend, jolting our husbands and boyfriends out of taking us for granted."

Sophie was immensely pleased that no-one thought the action was wasted. In fact, it seemed to have generated a great esprit de corps amongst the staff. She was welcomed back by everyone and given instant and friendly cooperation on the rearranged workload for the coming week.

There was so much to be done that Sophie and Jason worked right through until seven o'clock, leaving them only enough time to get to the airport an hour before their scheduled flight. Then it was rush, rush, rush to get seats confirmed and luggage checked. They no sooner arrived in the first-class waiting lounge than their boarding call was announced.

It was with a huge sense of relief that Sophie entered the first-class cabin. The tensions of the past week and the exhausting pace of the day's work seemed to slide away as a steward greeted them and ushered them to their seats. Jason offered her the choice of sitting next to the window and Sophie gratefully accepted, delighted to have the opportunity of enjoying whatever sights there were. She relaxed into the luxurious comfort of her seat and gave a deep sigh of pleasure.

"Happy now?" Jason asked, slanting her a friendly smile.

"Yes, thank you," she replied, wondering if his smile meant he was shedding the formal face of authority he had worn all day.

The steward served them champagne and Jason lifted his glass in a toast to her, a gleam of amusement dancing in his silver-grey eyes. "Have you always had such an impact on other people's lives?"

"I don't know what you mean," Sophie quickly defended.

One dark eyebrow lifted. "My scalp, and ten heads of red hair? Not to mention Evonne Carstairs's toes and my mother's soft heart? You are a force to be reckoned with, Sophie Melville."

"The hair wasn't my idea," she replied.

"It didn't have to be. I'm beginning to think you have a rippling effect that once started, proves unstoppable. God knows where it's going to end."

"It was your choice to rehire me," Sophie pointed out.

"I'm not complaining, Sophie. Merely making an observation." His eyes flicked over the bright sunburst of curls that framed her face. "I should have known I was playing with fire when I hired you in the first place. This is what I get for ignoring omens."

"But the omens were favourable, remember?"

"With some little help from you."

"Are you regretting taking me on again, Jason?"

"No," he said decisively. Then leaned back and laughed. "At the very least, it's made for an interesting week. And I expect this next week to be even more interesting."

Sophie relaxed again, feeling secure that her job was not under any threat from anything that had happened so far. "You haven't yet told me what part you want me to play in your scheme when we get to Bora Bora."

"It's a very delicate situation," he warned.

"I appreciate that."

"More delicate than you realise," he said grimly. "I'll want you to listen. Pick up vibrations. Watch body language. Advise me on whatever you think Gail is thinking and feeling. We have to find out if a rapprochement is possible before Randy arrives."

Sophie was secretly thrilled by the way Jason was linking her to him in partnership. This was precisely what she wanted.

"However, the prime requisite, before anything else can become possible," Jason continued with grave emphasis, "is to make it very clear to Gail that I cannot be used to make Randy jealous."

"Is it likely that she'd try to do that?"

"In her present volatile mood, she could seize any weapon to hurt him with. Including me. Especially me." He grimaced in distaste. "Gail has to see, and be convinced that such a move is impossible. And there must be no doubt about that in Randy's mind, either. Otherwise my effectiveness will be totally cancelled."

"Is this because you and Gail were lovers before she married Randy?" Sophie asked, seizing the opportunity to have that question cleared up.

He looked sharply at her, his face suddenly guarded, as though she had struck a highly sensitive nerve. "Six steps ahead of me again, Sophie?"

"If you want me to be effective for you, it's better that I know the facts," she argued as lightly as she could. "I've heard that you had a long-standing affair with her. Is it true or not?"

"It's true," he conceded reluctantly, his eyes flashing a bitter resentment of its being the subject of public gossip.

Sophie winced, hating to have to press the issue but not wanting to live in any uncertainty about it. "Did she end it, or did you?"

"I guess you could say Randy ended it," he said wryly. "It was obvious that they were better suited, what with their joint career taking off and the time they had for each other. I wished them well."

No rancour? No regrets? Sophie wondered. "And now? What do you feel for her now, Jason?" she asked quietly.

"You can't turn back the clock," he said with flat decisiveness. "I'll always be very fond of Gail. Impossible not to be. But I no longer want any intimate involvement with her."

Or with anyone? Sophie wondered. Was that why he picked up with women like Evonne Carstairs, deliberately eschewing any deep involvement? He might still be in love with Gail, while recognising that she had never felt for him what she felt for her husband. The passion there ran very deep for them to be acting so destructively.

"So how are you going to show Gail you're off-limits?" Sophie asked.

"With your help, it's very simple." The grey eyes locked onto hers, purpose flowing from him and winding inexorably around Sophie's heart and mind. "She has to be convinced you and I are lovers."

CHAPTER EIGHT

SOPHIE HEARD the powerful engines of the huge
jumbo jet thrum into action. It was too late for her to
abort the trip now, and Jason knew it.

She turned her head away from him, ostensibly to
watch and pay attention to the safety procedures
playing on the movie screen at the front of the cabin.
Sophie had heard them all before many times. She did
not need to be instructed again. Some clear strain of
logic in her mind kept working, ignoring the emotional turmoil that swirled around it. Like a movie reel
in her brain, it clicked through the sequence of events
that had led up to this moment.

Her solution to the Sullivan wrangle had been the
starting point. But that had been unworkable unless
Jason produced a convincing lover at his side. Obviously he had not wanted to use Evonne Carstairs.
Evonne undoubtedly would have tried to turn a convenience into a claim. So what he needed was a woman
who would serve his purpose and was easily cast off
afterwards.

Hence the month's trial for Sophie, who was perfect for the part. He was doing her the favour of a
high-salaried job for a month, and a free first-class

trip to one of the most beautiful tropical islands in the world. Unfortunately all that had blown up in his face last Friday.

Then it was a case of Operation Rescue. The extravagant apologies, the agony money, the clothes money, leaving no stone unturned to get his plan back on course, to bend her to his will. Perhaps the plan looked even better because there was no denying a physical attraction between them. He had subtly tested that again on their walk home from the restaurant.

Her inward churning over his outrageous assumption that she would play along with the lovers scheme gradually simmered to a controllable level as Sophie began to consider if there was any chance left for a future between them. Jason was attracted to her. He was treating her as more of an equal than an underling. Perhaps she was clinging to the hope of the hopeless, but something in her heart begged her to leave everything open until she had more information.

The safety film finished playing. The steward handed them dinner menus and Sophie pretended to study the choices as the plane taxied to its runway for take-off. She was conscious of Jason watching her, patiently waiting for her reaction, probably plotting persuasive responses to any protests she might make. Let him wait, she thought, fiercely resenting the way he had held back on her to ensure a favourable position for himself.

When she felt the plane lift off, she closed the menu and looked out the window. This was always the best moment, she thought, the sense of flying away on a new adventure. She watched the lights of Sydney spread out below her, far far below, and wondered if the adventure she was now embarked on would change her life in any significant way. So much depended on the man sitting beside her.

"Sophie..." His patience had obviously run out. The tension in his voice begged some response from her. Any response. He needed something to work on.

She turned to face him, her eyes meeting his in cool challenge. "I've been thinking of the time and effort you've expended in getting me here. The money you've shelled out on dressing me for the part." She paused, then softly added, "This must mean a lot to you, Jason."

He frowned, not expecting such perception from her. His mouth slowly curled into a sardonic little smile. "I don't like untidy endings."

"Neither do I," she said with feeling. Their week together on Bora Bora should sort out what ending they would come to. She offered him a sympathetic smile. "I'll give you all the help you need."

His relief was almost comical until it gave way to a look of speculative calculation on how far she might go in helping him. "I'm glad you see it my way," he said with admirable restraint.

Now for the pay back, Sophie thought, determined that Jason should stew in the scheme he had kept to himself. "It's easy for me," she tripped out, her blue eyes limpid with innocence. "I presume you do realise that in order for your purpose to be achieved, I don't have to pretend to be in love with you."

"You're already in love with me?" he asked incredulously.

She laughed. "Of course not! How could I be? You're not thinking straight, Jason. It's not necessary for me to appear besotted with you. Gail and Randy won't care about what I feel. It's what you feel that matters. To bring this off, *you* have to appear besotted with *me*. I can simply be myself. Whom you adore to distraction."

He looked decidedly ruffled by this argument.

Sophie's eyes twinkled teasingly at him as she rubbed it in. "Do you think you can manage to deliver that? Follow me around as though you can't bear to have me out of touch, let alone out of sight? Keep looking at me as though I'm the most desirable woman in the world? React slavishly to my every word?"

Such a one-sided role did not sit well with his male ego. He frowned, not at all happy with the picture Sophie had drawn. "This could blow up in our faces," he muttered.

"It's your scheme, Jason. The onus of making it convincing is entirely on your shoulders." She laughed with a delicious ripple of anticipation. "I imagine it will be quite a lot of fun for me."

Her amusement was sheer poison to him. The grey eyes glittered with storm signals. "I'll have to think about this," he said grimly.

"Fine! It certainly sounds like a good scheme to me, but let me know if you want to change something when you've thought it all through. In the meantime, I'll just sit back and enjoy myself. Super food they're offering, isn't it?" she added blithely, opening her menu.

The food was indeed splendid. Sophie ate her way through some appetisers, caviar with all its embellishments, a little glass of vodka, a garden salad, exquisitely tender and tasty roast beef with vegetables, a fine selection of cheeses and a chocolate mousse with cream.

Jason, she noticed, had very little appetite for any of his meal. Serves him right, Sophie thought, her sense of justice appeased. He had ruined her appetite for the meal at Pommeroys Restaurant.

He showed no appetite for watching the movie, either. Or listening to any music. He didn't bother with his earphones at all. Sophie left him to his thinking and happily immersed herself in the story on screen, which was a good enough comedy to make her laugh several times. When it was over, she levered her wonderfully roomy seat back to its lowest reclining position and snuggled down for a few hours' sleep.

She must have dozed off for a while because when her eyes flicked open sometime later, Jason's seat was aligned with hers and he was staring at her as though trying to plumb what made her the way she was.

"Can't you sleep?" she asked kindly, hiding the satisfaction she felt at his puzzlement.

"Perhaps I need a goodnight kiss," he said, giving her a tempting little smile.

Sophie heaved a sigh to still the treacherous flutter in her heart, then closed her eyes again. "Must be missing Evonne," she muttered derisively.

She heard his sigh of frustration and felt justice had been served once again. If he had thought about seducing her into the kind of convenient relationship he had shared with his last social connection, he could think again. Chemistry could be exciting, but Sophie had no intention of becoming a dispensable bed partner.

She drifted back to sleep and did not wake again until the cabin lights came on prior to their landing in Tahiti. Jason was not in his seat. Stealing a march on one of the toilets, she thought, and stirred herself to do the same.

Having tidied and refreshed herself, Sophie returned to her seat to find Jason and a cup of coffee waiting for her. "Good morning," she said with a sunny smile, then sat down and looked out the window at the rising sun. "It's going to be a fine day."

"Sophie, we need to talk about this scheme," Jason said tersely, demanding her attention.

"Oh, right!" She swung around to face him with another bright smile, inviting the fruit of his thoughts.

Although he had shaved and his general appearance was immaculate, he looked quite haggard around the eyes and somewhat pinched around his mouth. Sophie almost felt sorry for him. But he had to learn she was not a stupid bunny to be manipulated any way he liked. Not with money, nor with sex appeal.

"I can't carry it off without your co-operation," he stated, the grey eyes piercingly intense as they searched hers for any wavering from her previous stand on the lovers scheme.

"I'm a reasonable person," Sophie assured him. "If what you want is reasonable, Jason, I'll certainly oblige."

"Both Gail and Randy know that I'm not a masochistic fool. It would be unbelievable to them for me to be besotted with a woman who appears to be indifferent to me. At the very least I'll need some show of encouragement from you."

Sophie nodded her understanding. "You're right. A man who calculates things out as cold-bloodedly as you do is not going to get hot-blooded unless he thinks he has a chance of winning."

He frowned at this reading of his character.

"How much encouragement do you think would be reasonable?" Sophie asked, frowning in sympathetic consideration.

His eyes glittered at her with some inward seething, and Sophie had the satisfaction of knowing she was well and truly under his skin at the present moment.

"Can you look as though you enjoy being touched by me?" he asked in a somewhat acid tone.

"Depends on the kind of touch," Sophie answered matter-of-factly, then raised her eyebrows at him. "I trust you don't go in for taking distasteful liberties in public?"

"Not my style," he assured her.

"In that case, I won't mind playing along with the touching." She grinned at him. "I'll give you an objective sensuality rating when this is over, if you like."

A low growl rumbled in his throat. He took a deep breath to clear the gravelly obstruction but didn't quite succeed. "A few kisses might be in order," he rasped.

Sophie shrugged. "I guess a week in paradise would seem lacking without the odd kiss or two. I'll do my best to whip up the appropriate fervour for them."

"Thank you," he drawled, barely missing bitter sarcasm. "I hope it won't strain your obliging nature too far."

She eyed him speculatively. "Are you good at it?"

"I've never had any complaints."

"Well, it'll be interesting to see if age improves technique. I've never had anyone as old as you as a lover before."

"I'm not that old!" he bit out.

"I didn't say you were too old," Sophie soothed. "Only that—"

"I heard you the first time," he said in terse exasperation.

She gave him a worried look. "This isn't going to rebound on my job, is it, Jason? I mean, you have rather landed this scheme on me, and I don't think it falls within the normal course of duties for a personal assistant. Being a pretend lover wasn't in the required qualifications. I can only do my best—"

"Sophie!" He looked driven to the limits of his endurance. His eyes flashed a hot challenge. "You said you were prepared for anything."

"Yes, I did. You're absolutely right," she agreed. "I'll give it my best shot. I just hope you're not going to blame me for some failure of yours. That wouldn't be fair."

"I am not going to fail," he stated with vehement determination.

"Fine! That's it, then. I'm to give the appropriate encouragement for you to be utterly besotted," Sophie recited, then smiled up at the steward who was about to serve them breakfast.

Forty minutes later they were disembarking at Faaa Airport and breathing in the balmy air of the tropics. Although it was only six-thirty in the morning, it was hot and humid enough for Jason to feel uncomfortable in his suit. Since they had to wait an hour for their flight to Bora Bora, which lay two hundred and seventy kilometres to the northwest of Tahiti, he left Sophie at the airport café and went off to change his clothes.

Having never seen Jason in anything but a business suit, Sophie suffered a considerable shock to her sys-

tem when she saw him stripped of his formal finery.
The classy executive suddenly emerged as a strikingly
attractive male, complete with bronzed muscles and a
physique that needed no padding by a master tailor.
He wore a royal blue Henley-style top and cotton
pants, printed in greys and blues and washed to a
comfortable well-worn fade. Every woman seated in
the café looked him over with admiration and interest.

Sophie learnt a new appreciation of chemistry and
biology as Jason sat down next to her and gave her a
dazzling smile. "That feels better," he said.

"Looks more the part, as well," Sophie replied
dryly. As a pretend lover, he certainly came with the
kind of masculine equipment that made pretence easy.
At least on the surface. Sophie concentrated hard on
remembering that substance was far more important.

"Two hours to blast-off," he remarked with the air
of a man who was not looking forward to the task he
had set himself. He flicked a wary look at her. "I hope
you're ready for it."

"No problem," she answered lightly.

Control was the name of the game, she told herself
sternly. Cast-iron control! If she once let him past her
guard, Sophie had the distinct feeling that Jason
would have no scruples about going for the jugular, if
only in retaliation for what she had put him through.

He slept throughout the hour's flight to Bora Bora.
Sophie was tempted to wake him to share the breath-
taking sight of the island from the air, but she forced

herself to remain businesslike. A good assistant would let her boss restore the energy he would undoubtedly need for the job ahead of him.

Nevertheless, he missed out on a fabulous sight. The island was almost completely surrounded and protected by a barrier reef onto which the ocean waves crashed and spurted up white foam. Within the reef, the water was an opalescent green, contrasting sharply with the deep blue without and creating a jewel-like setting for the island itself.

The spectacular land formation was clearly of volcanic origin, and huge craggy peaks dominated a mountain chain that ran along the major axis of the island. The deep green of the vegetation looked lushly tropical, as did the masses of palm trees crowding the coastline. It all looked wonderfully untouched by civilisation, a special place existing apart and totally unspoiled, a monument of beauty that nature had created and adorned with unique and loving care.

Sophie had seen many wonderful sights in her travels, but none like this. She understood now why it was called the *fabled* Bora Bora. Of all the islands in the Pacific, none could compare with the grandeur of its lagoon or the majesty of its peaks. It was the home of the Polynesian culture, and from its shores had sailed the longboats that had taken its people to colonise the thousands of islands throughout the world's largest ocean.

It made Sophie feel privileged to be here, and she knew that this magical place would live in her memory forever, no matter what happened in the coming week.

Jason woke as the plane touched down on the coral atoll of Motu Mute, where U.S. forces had built the airstrip in 1943 as an integral part of their naval base in the South Pacific. "Only the launch ride to go now, and then we'll be at the hotel," Sophie said with bright anticipation, resolving to enjoy all she could while she was here. "I hope you're going to be ready for it, Jason," she added, eyeing his bleary state with misgivings.

"No problem," he muttered.

But he dozed off again in the luxurious motor launch as it sped over the lagoon and across the deepwater harbour to the Hotel Bora Bora on Pointe Raititi. Sophie marvelled at the incredible clarity of the water that now seemed more turquoise than green. They passed the small village of Vaitape and several other tourist resorts. They were all constructed in the native style, the guest accommodation consisting of individual *farés* with pandanus leaf roofs. Many of these were built out over the water, since there was little land between the coastal road and the lagoon.

Jason stirred himself to life as the launch slowed for its approach to the hotel dock. He shook off his air of fatigue and practised a besotted look at Sophie, who burst into giggles from sheer nervous tension.

"This isn't going to work," Jason grated, affronted by her reaction to his first effort at acting.

"Oh, loosen up, Jason," Sophie advised. "Lovers do laugh at each other, you know."

It teased a rueful smile from him. "It's been a long time since I felt like a lover."

"Well, if you will waste your life on women like Evonne Carstairs, I expect that would stultify any honest emotions."

"Sometimes it's easier to live without emotions. But I expect you're too young to know that," he said flatly.

"No, I'm not, Jason. But cutting off one's emotional life is a very dehumanising thing to do. It leads to not caring about what other people feel."

He grimaced. "You're beginning to sound like my mother."

She smiled. "I like your mother."

A look of wry appreciation flashed into his eyes. "She likes you, too."

Yes, she does, Sophie thought, which didn't gel with the fact that Mrs. Whitlow had been privy to Jason's scheme of getting Sophie to Bora Bora with him, and dressing her for the part he wanted her to play. She had also witnessed the jolt Sophie had given her son's self-image, and admired its delivery. Perhaps Mrs. Whitlow wanted Sophie to deliver a few more jolts. In which case, she must believe Jason had a good heart, to be tapped if only someone could reach it, and she was counting on Sophie as the most likely candidate.

Of course, his mother might be wrong about the good heart. It might have shrivelled up and died since

Gail's defection to Randy. On the other hand, Jason was certainly able to feel emotion. He had demonstrated that several times with her. Which had to mean she tapped something inside him, whether he liked it or not. Something more than physical chemistry.

Sophie's heart lightened considerably throughout this train of thought. She gave Jason an encouraging smile as the launch was brought to a halt beside the dock. "Just hold my hand and smile indulgently at me while I admire everything about the hotel. That will get you started on the right track."

He laughed and took both her hands to draw her up beside him, and together they stepped onto the quay of the Hotel Bora Bora.

"Paradise!" Sophie breathed in pure delight at all that met her eyes.

"Lost or regained?" Jason murmured.

"Neither!" Sophie grinned at him. "Paradise found, of course!"

"I hope it ends up that way," he said fervently.

"Come, Jason! Where's your confidence?" she chided, her eyes laughingly mocking him.

He sighed. "Unfortunately, there's a couple of surprises still in the offing."

"Like what?"

"I think it might be best if we wait until we come to them," he said, and tried very hard to smile indulgently.

CHAPTER NINE

THE *FARÉ* WAS perfectly situated. From the front porch there were a few metres of manicured lawn to the beach, then a few metres of white sand to the warm waters of the lagoon. A double hammock hung on the palm trees just beyond the front porch, and two reclining sun lounges awaited the occupants' convenience.

Sophie would normally be thrilled out of her mind to have accommodation in such a glorious position. Her pleasure, however, was considerably diminished by one of Jason's surprises. Although it was not specifically stated, she was left in no doubt that she was supposed to be sharing the *faré* with him.

Their luggage was carried in and set up on stands for easy unpacking. They were shown the facilities in the kitchenette-cum-dressing-room as though they were a couple. They were both invited to check out the bathroom. The only other room was the one they had entered, a very spacious living area containing two double beds, a dining setting, two chests of drawers and two armchairs. They were wished a very happy stay at the Hotel Bora Bora and left to settle in together.

Sophie marched straight to the door and flung it wide open to the front porch. With her exit route made emphatically clear, she swung around to hurl a seething challenge at the man who had organised this cosy arrangement.

"What made you think I would accept this set-up?"

He remained near their luggage, as though guarding it might stop her from storming out on him. His hands lifted in appeal. "Sophie, it's not as bad as it looks," he started apologetically.

"Crass, Jason!" she fired at him. "Very, very crass! Did you imagine I would be flattered?"

"No. I—"

"That I would happily seize the chance of sharing so much intimacy with you?"

He looked intensely discomfited. He had obviously figured that she wouldn't mind too much.

"That you could always buy my compliance with a few more thousand dollars?" she taunted.

"I've never bought a woman in my life!" he rasped, affronted by the very idea.

"Were you skimping on costs, then?"

Red slashed across his cheekbones. "No!"

"So what wonderful line of reasoning went through your mind, Jason?"

"I couldn't get an adjoining *faré* for you," he snapped. "You know damned well our schedule had to be pushed forward. What was available starting next weekend was not available for this week. It's a simple matter of logistics, Sophie."

"There isn't another vacant *faré* at the hotel? Is that what you're saying, Jason?"

"Sure, there is!" He waved his hands in exasperation. "Back in the garden somewhere. Not on the beach front. And not close by. How do you think it would look for me, in this day and age, to bring a woman here and have her parked nowhere near me?"

"So your male pride is more important than my sensibilities, is it?" Sophie demanded acidly.

"I'm only thinking of the situation!" he insisted. "If it upsets you so much, I'll sleep in the hammock outside and you can have the place to yourself. But we have to at least look as though we're together."

He did have a point, Sophie acknowledged. "You truly booked an adjoining *faré* for me in the first place?" she queried.

"Yes. And you can easily check that out if you don't believe me," he added bitterly.

"Am I still going to hold my job after a week of togetherness with you, Jason? Or are you figuring on getting rid of me?" she asked point-blank.

He dragged in a deep breath and expelled a long, shaky sigh. "How can I get rid of you, Sophie? With this set of circumstances, you could nail me to a wall, if I tried. I've given you my deepest confidence, and I'm trusting to your integrity to keep whatever happens this week to yourself."

He was certainly a good advocate, she thought. His voice fairly throbbed with sincerity, and what he said did make sense. Since several major considerations had been cleared up to her satisfaction, Sophie decided she could let the matter rest for the time being.

"Well, at least there are separate beds," she observed, then stepped over to the one closest to the door and dropped her carry bag onto it. "I'll take this one."

"Do I dare assume that I may use the other?" Jason asked, cautious about taking anything for granted after the diatribe he had just been subjected to.

Sophie gave a sigh of resigned sufferance. "I guess it wouldn't look too good if Gail or Randy spotted you sleeping in the hammock every night. Just remember the pretence-lover bit stops at that door."

"Of course," he soothed. "Thank you for your understanding, Sophie."

She shot him a dark look. "I hope you don't snore."

His mouth twitched into a dry little smile. "You could always beat me over the head with a pillow. With the beatings I've been taking lately, that should put me out for the count."

Sophie could barely repress a responding smile. She quickly turned her head aside, working to retain a stern composure while appearing to be checking out the view through the doorway.

She was about to ask what other surprises Jason had kept up his sleeve when her attention was drawn to a woman crossing the lawn from the adjacent *faré*. Sophie took one sharp look at her, knew there was no time to waste in setting up Jason's scheme and took the initiative upon herself. To his stunned surprise she whirled down the room, flinging herself at him and throwing her arms around his neck.

"This is going to be heavenly, darling! Thank you so much for bringing me here!" she cried out loud, looking at him fatuously as she quickly hissed, "Kiss me!"

She had to say one thing for Jason. He was not slow on the uptake. His arms came around her like a vice. "My pleasure," he said with a passionate throb that smacked of real feeling, and when his mouth came down on hers, he certainly couldn't be accused of not being convincing.

Sophie wasn't sure if he was working off all the ego burns she had given him, or whether the thought of Gail witnessing his passion for another woman was the driving force, but she was left in little doubt about his expertise at kissing and his ability to put it all into practice in one fell swoop.

His lips moved over hers with a hungry sensuality that stunned her into giving way to each seductive pressure. She felt his hand slide into her hair, fingers persuading the tilt of her head as his mouth sought for more complete access to hers. She gave it unthinkingly, fascinated by the promise of knowing more of him, more of how it might feel together if she let it happen.

Somewhere in the back of her mind she knew it was safe because Gail was coming. But she forgot all about Gail when Jason's tongue started an erotic sweep over hers. Electric tingles jammed her brain, and all com-

mon sense was lost as he plunged her down a path of
sensation that stirred a mindless range of responses
throughout her body.

"Jason!"

Gail Sullivan's shocked cry came in the nick of time,
Sophie realised afterwards. Control had suffered a
complete meltdown. She found her fingers entwined
in Jason's hair when he lifted his head, and the way
her body was strained to meet every part of his was a
dead giveaway. Or a live one, considering the zinging
palpitation in her nerves and the wild acceleration of
her heartbeat, not to mention the rivulets of weak-
ness in her legs and the prickling sensitivity of her
breasts. Chemical dynamite, Sophie thought dazedly,
and didn't dare look up at Jason as he greeted their
visitor.

"Gail . . ." His voice sounded thick. He tried clear-
ing his throat, but Gail Sullivan forestalled any further utterance.

"I can't believe this!" she screeched in outrage.
"You conned me into coming all this way. I've come
to welcome you. And your first priority is to get some
floozy into bed with you!"

Floozy jarred Sophie into movement. As she shifted
to face her detractor, Jason reacted automatically,
tucking her beside him with one arm while gesturing
appeasement at Gail with the other.

"You've got this wrong, Gail. Sophie is not a—"

"You're no better than Randy! Worse!" came the swift and bitter condemnation, her large amber eyes flaring fire and brimstone.

Gail Sullivan had far more vital charisma in the flesh than was ever seen in her photographs, and fury gave her a wild vividness that heightened every feature of her natural beauty. Sophie's heart quivered uncertainly as she took in the glorious shiny mane of creamy caramel hair, the flawless skin that was flushed with rage, the superbly arched eyebrows, the aristocratic nose with the flare of passion breathing from her nostrils, the perfectly sculptured mouth, the long graceful neck stretched taut with wounded pride and the lissome body seductively draped in a multicoloured pareu. Unforgettable, Sophie thought, and no longer wondered about Jason's failure to find any woman to compare with her.

"If you'll listen for a moment—" Jason tried again.

"I thought you were the one man I could trust!" Gail flung at him. "So much for old friendships! You're fired!" With a contemptuous toss of her head, she turned her back on both of them and marched off in high dudgeon.

"Wait!" Jason's appeal fell on deaf ears.

"Hell hath no fury like a woman scorned," Sophie observed.

Jason hissed some curse under his breath, then disengaged himself from Sophie as though she were contaminated. "You overdid it!" he accused.

Sophie stared at him in disbelief. "I only started it. It was you who overdid it."

"You caught me by surprise, responding as you did after giving me to believe—"

"Well, you turned out to be a better kisser than I thought you would," she defended wildly.

His eyes glittered with a turbulent range of emotions. "Will you stop turning me inside out, Sophie? I don't know where the hell I am with you."

"Try being fair."

He looked at her mutinous expression, then shook his head in frustration. "Nothing works with you, does it?"

"Wrong strategy. And you blew it with Gail, as well," Sophie retaliated.

His face set in grim determination. "I have to go after her."

"If you want her back, you'll certainly have to do that," Sophie agreed.

"God help me!" he muttered as he headed for the door. "I'm between the devil and the deep blue sea!"

"Good luck," Sophie called after him.

At least she had the satisfaction of knowing that Gail was not about to fall into Jason's arms. In fact, Sophie assured herself, she had every reason to be highly pleased with the results of her initiative. Not only had it put Gail off any idea of a more than friendly reunion with Jason, it had also confirmed that Jason was not entirely play-acting his role of lover.

Sophie was quite sure he had been as much involved as she in finding out how a kiss between them felt. If he hadn't lost track of his original purpose, he would have been more prepared to meet Gail's interruption. Which gave Sophie cause for hope, despite the formidable competition of the living reminder of Jason's lost love.

Since she was definitely persona non grata in the Sullivan camp until some kind of peace treaty was reached, Sophie figured that her job, in keeping with Jason's scheme, was to be as flamboyantly conspicuous as possible, driving the point home that she was not going to go away. She was a fixture in Jason's life, whether Gail liked it or not, and until Jason instructed her otherwise, that was how she was going to act.

She quickly unpacked her clothes, selected the bandeau swimsuit and its matching pareu for her first appearance on stage, then stripped off and smothered her skin with a block-out lotion to protect it from the sun's harmful rays. Although Jason had listed bikinis, Sophie had been unable to resist the marvellous colour combination of the dramatic one-piece with its brilliant sea-green bust line, the wide purple waistband with the mirrored insets of green and blue and the electric blue lower half that was cut almost to the hips to give the longest of long-legged looks.

She picked up the pareu and one of the beach towels provided, then strolled down to the stretch of beach directly in front of Gail's *faré*. Out of the corner of her eye she saw Jason and Gail in verbal confrontation on her front porch, but Sophie did not pause or glance their way.

There was a number of recliners set out along the sand. She spent some time relaxing on one of them, enjoying the light breeze that took any sting out of the tropical heat, drinking in the fabulous ambience around her, idly observing other guests who strolled by. Eventually she decided a swim was in order, particularly since it gave her a natural opportunity to look around and see if Jason had made any progress with Gail.

The water was wonderful, cool enough to be refreshing, warm enough to caress her skin like the softest silk. It was so clear, the occasional rock or coral outcrop could easily be avoided underfoot, and to Sophie's fascinated delight, she could see fish darting around her. Some looked transparent, merging with the water, but others were brilliantly coloured in bold stripes or beautiful rainbow tints that seemed to flow into each other with an iridescent glow.

Jason and Gail had apparently reached some kind of truce for they progressed to sitting around a small table set on the lawn outside her *faré*, sipping drinks and conversing with some intensity. Sophie caught Jason glancing her way a couple of times, but Gail seemed intent on ignoring her existence.

The swim stirred Sophie's appetite. She waded out of the lagoon, dried herself with the beach towel, tied the pareu around her waist, then waited to catch Jason's eye. She waved an indication of where he could find her, then at his nod of acknowledgement set off for the Pofai Beach Bar on the other side of the point.

Sophie had a hamburger and a Chi Chi cocktail, struck up an acquaintance with two American couples who were both on their honeymoon, found out that the hotel supplied complimentary snorkelling equipment and lessons on how to use it and generally idled away the afternoon chatting with the lovely Polynesian bar attendants who were only too happy to tell her about their life on Bora Bora.

She saw nothing of Jason or Gail for the rest of the day. Where they went and what they did were not communicated to her by word or message. They did not attend the beach barbecue that evening, and Sophie was left completely to her own devices.

She told herself that the business with Gail had to come first with Jason. That was why they were here. But it didn't stop her from feeling left out and lonely and miserable at the thought of Gail wielding her formidable female power over Jason. Fortunately, the friendly Americans she had met invited her to sit with them, and they were such happy company that the hours passed pleasantly enough.

She was already in bed when Jason finally made a reappearance. He blundered into the *faré*, having missed the step from the porch, cursed under his breath, then fumbled around in the dark, trying to find his way noiselessly to the bathroom. Sophie heaved a great sigh and snapped on the bedside lamp.

"Sorry if I woke you," he said, looking so haggard and wrung out that Sophie swallowed back the caustic comment trembling on her tongue.

"Trying day?" she asked sympathetically.

He looked grateful for her understanding. "Then some," he said with feeling. "I can't get through to Gail at all. Not on any level."

"How many levels did you try?"

The jealous snipe slid out before Sophie could stop it, and she felt intensely mortified. Jason had told her categorically that he didn't want an intimate relationship with Gail. Because the other woman was so unnervingly beautiful, and they had spent so much time alone together, it didn't necessarily mean he had changed his mind about what he wanted.

Jason gave her a bleak look. "I tried everything I could think of. I'm sorry I can't include you, Sophie. I could use some advice. But Gail has taken an irrational dislike to you."

She gave a dismissive shrug, relieved that he was too tired to perceive her own irrational feelings. "It's your scheme. If you want me out, I'm out. Though it would be nice to know when to dress up or not. If I'd known I had the evening off, I needn't have wasted a snazzy pyjama suit on a beach barbecue."

His mouth curled with irony. "It wasn't wasted. Gail didn't fancy a barbecue so I took her to the yacht club on the other side of the village. Before we left here we had a drink in the Matira Bar, which overlooks the beach. Gail commented, somewhat waspishly, that you seemed very adept at picking up people."

"A knack I learnt from travelling alone," Sophie answered lightly, relieved to hear they had gone out for dinner instead of being closeted in Gail's *faré*. "I guess it's more of the same tomorrow."

"That's how it stands at the moment."

"Oh, well! Sorry I can't help." She gave him a commiserating smile. "You look dead beat, Jason. Better get some sleep." She settled herself in bed and turned her back to him. "You can turn out the light when you're ready."

He didn't move for several moments. Sophie could feel him staring at her. Then she heard him strip off his clothes. She knew he hadn't unpacked, and he didn't bother doing it now. He used the bathroom, then climbed into bed and switched off the lamp.

She couldn't help wondering if he had gone to bed stark naked. It was a disturbing image. It was an even more disturbing image when he tossed and turned, apparently too wound up from the long confrontation with Gail to relax into a peaceful sleep. Or perhaps he was suffering from exhaustion, his nerves twitching out of control. Whatever the reason, his restlessness continued for over an hour, and when he punched his pillows into a different shape for the umpteenth time, Sophie decided she couldn't stand it anymore. She slid out of bed, picked up the towel and bikini she had laid out ready for a morning swim and quietly opened the door.

"Where are you going?"

The gruff bark from him halted her in mid-exit. "I think I'd prefer it if you snored," she said bluntly. "It's impossible to sleep with a threshing machine in the next bed, so I'm going for a swim. Maybe you'll be dead to the world when I come back."

There was no-one on the beach. Sophie stepped into the bikini bottom and pulled it up under her cotton nightie. Then she tossed off her nightie, picked up the bikini bra and was about to fasten it around her breasts when the lure of the moonlit lagoon changed her mind.

Why not swim topless? Many of the guests had been sunbathing topless today. It was customary and commonplace in France and other overseas territories. The Polynesians accepted it as part of their cultural heritage. Sophie was not quite that uninhibited about her body, but there was nothing to stop her from enjoying the sensual freedom of swimming like that tonight.

She dropped the bra onto her towel and ran into the water, undeterred by its initial coolness. As soon as it was deep enough she immersed herself in a long glide that felt delicious against her bare skin. After a few languorous strokes she turned onto her back to float, enjoying the sensation of little waves lapping over the peaks of her breasts. The boom of league-long rollers pounding on the coral reef vibrated through her ears. The sky was full of stars. Magic, she thought. Pure magic.

There was a small eruption of water beside her. Sophie idly thought of fish jumping until Jason's voice shattered that sweet delusion.

"Are you all right, Sophie?"

She flapped her arms and thrust her feet down in a frantic bid to move away from him. "You're supposed to be sleeping!" she cried, fiercely protesting his intrusion on her private idyll with nature.

"You should know better than to go swimming alone at night. You could hurt your feet on a rock, get cramp..."

"In water this warm?" she scoffed. "As for rocks, if you look down you can see the dark blobs for yourself. I'm perfectly safe in this lagoon."

He looked down, but his gaze fastened on her breasts and didn't lower any farther. She lifted her hands to cover herself. "I wasn't expecting you to follow me, Jason," she pleaded.

"You're so beautiful," he murmured. "Don't hide yourself, Sophie." He reached out and gently drew her hands away. "I thought you would look like this," he said huskily.

"Don't," she whispered, her breath catching in her throat at the breaking of barriers between them. She hastily pushed herself away from him, making a safer space, frightened of her vulnerability to his touch.

He made no move to follow her but his eyes clung to hers, compelling her attention. "You feel it, too," he said. "It's been waiting to happen since last Friday. Before that. So why not let it, Sophie?"

His devastating directness caught her unprepared, and she was at a loss as to how to answer him. "Friday was the day you hurt me," she reminded him, fighting the almost magnetic pull of his attraction.

"Can't it be different now?" he asked softly.

"You planned to use me all along. How can I know you wouldn't be using me now, Jason? Perhaps to put Gail out of your mind, and all you once shared with her? You must have been remembering that today. Remembering..."

"No. I wanted to be with you."

"But you weren't. You didn't even leave me a message to say where you were. I was nothing."

"You know why we came to Bora Bora," he said.

"I did what you wanted of me, and you cut me off. I was very lonely."

"We're together now."

"Only because you kept on punching your pillows."

"To stop myself from reaching out to you."

How did one fight truth? Desire throbbed from his voice, beating relentlessly on a responsive chord that Sophie recognised only too well. The torment of being so aware of him in the next bed had kept her awake, too, driven her away from him. She was suddenly riven with the thought that he was naked, that he hadn't bothered with a swimsuit when he followed her.

Her gaze dropped to his shoulders gleaming bare in the moonlight, the strongly delineated maleness of his chest, then to the wavering waterline. No, she thought, I have to stop this, and forced herself to turn away from him and face the reef. Her mind was a jumbled mess of needs and desires. Impossible to pluck any smart, sensible words out of it. She felt the movement in the water, knew what it meant, yet could not find the will to evade the danger it forewarned.

His arms slid around her waist and slowly drew her against him. "Let it be," he murmured, his mouth grazing softly near her ear.

"Let it be what, Jason?" Her voice was thin and uncertain, barely recognisable as her own. "An affair to remember?" she forced out. "Or a convenience to be forgotten?"

His hands glided up to close possessively around her breasts. She felt his chest expand as he breathed in hard, then in a fervent whisper that blew softly through her curls he said, "I want you very badly, Sophie. More than I've wanted any woman I've ever met."

He trailed a mesmerising line of kisses down her throat, across her shoulders. Sophie tried to think, but her senses were being stormed by the sweet seduction of the man behind her and the balmy romance of the elements around them, the softness of the water lapping their bodies, the strangely secure feeling of having her weightless breasts caressed, the sensuous feeling of wet warm flesh meeting and fitting together.

Somehow it stirred a kind of reckless fatalism. Her instincts whispered that this was how it should be, a sharing of what nature intended for man and woman without any need for promises or thought of the future. Perhaps the primitive magic of the fabled Bora Bora had seeped into her soul. Through her mind and her heart and her body ran the rhythmic refrain, *Let it be... let it be.*

When Jason turned her to face him she offered no resistance. Her body willingly met his, and she wound her arms around him and gave him kiss for kiss, and she clung to him unashamedly as he carried her out of the lagoon, wanting what he wanted, uncaring of tomorrow.

CHAPTER TEN

SOPHIE WAS WOKEN by a sharp rap on the *faré* door. It only took a moment for her to realise she was alone. The bed was cold where Jason had lain. There was no sound from the bathroom. He had left her to sleep on without him.

"Miss Melville," a voice lilted from outside.

"Yes? Come in," Sophie called, quickly dragging a sheet over her nakedness.

One of the Polynesian staff entered, her dark eyes flashing teasingly at the tumbled state of the bed as she grinned at Sophie and her ragged attempt at modesty. She carried a number of leis over her arm and she proceeded to set them out on the bed Sophie had vacated last night.

"Mr. Lombard said to bring you all these. They are to make you feel as beautiful as you are." The dark eyes sparkled with pleasure in the romantic message. "That's what he told me to tell you."

"Thank you," Sophie replied, both relieved and warmed by the gesture. She instinctively shied away from the thought that last night might have been a terrible mistake. It couldn't be. She wouldn't let it be, she thought wildly.

"Do you know where Mr. Lombard is now?" she asked.

"Gone on the *Vehia* with Mrs. Sullivan."

Sophie frowned. "What's the *Vehia*?"

"The big sailing boat. It takes guests on a picnic cruise around the lagoon. They will be gone all day."

Sophie heaved a sigh of disappointment, even though it was what she had to expect, given the situation with Gail.

"But Mr. Lombard, he is thinking of you, Miss Melville," the lei-bearer said archly as she made her exit, leaving Sophie on an uplifting note.

The problem was, Sophie did not really know what Jason thought of her, apart from wanting her very badly. Yet it was impossible to regret giving in to him last night. How often did the right person coincide with the right time and place for something uniquely special to happen?

It was a question that niggled at her mind all day. Jason would undoubtedly be anticipating that she would share his bed for the rest of their stay on Bora Bora, but with the way things were turning out, there wasn't going to be much other sharing. If any. Which reduced what was happening between them to a very sexual affair, and Sophie wanted far more than that.

Live for the day, a tempting little voice whispered in her head. Since it was impossible to go back, the only way was forward. *I will be happy, no matter what,* Sophie finally resolved.

It was a resolution she valiantly held to until she watched the *Vehia* come in from its cruise. She had settled on a sun lounger on Pointe Raititi for this very purpose, since it gave the most encompassing view of all that could be seen from the beach. The guests on the deck of the large catamaran looked happy and relaxed, as though they didn't have a care in the world. Sophie felt a deep stab of envy. They had all shared a companionable day while she waited on tenterhooks for what would happen next.

Pride insisted that she not appear to be waiting for anything. For all she knew, Jason would be with Gail for hours yet. She settled back on the lounger and closed her eyes, determined to be detached and aloof until she was given reason to be otherwise.

Nevertheless, she couldn't resist watching the path from the quay through the veil of her lashes. She wanted to see if Jason was holding Gail's hand, how they looked together. Perhaps it was stupid of her to feel threatened by their former relationship, but she couldn't help wondering how and when love died. She didn't want that to happen to her.

Her heart gave a kick of pleasurable relief when she saw Jason striding out ahead of the disembarking group. He had not waited to escort Gail anywhere. He must have spotted Sophie, been looking for her while he was still on board the *Vehia,* because his gaze was trained on her from the moment he came into sight.

He stopped at the Pofai Beach Bar, apparently to order drinks, but he kept his eye on Sophie, not once glancing to check on where Gail was. Sophie didn't bother checking, either. It didn't matter. Being the focus of Jason's attention was too marvellous a sensation to give up for anything.

He must have asked the bar attendant what she liked to drink. He carried a Chi Chi cocktail when he resumed his beeline for her. He was smiling, a look of happy anticipation on his face. Sophie stayed precisely where she was, pretending that she had not seen him, but every nerve in her body was singing with hope and pleasure.

"Sophie..." She fluttered her eyelashes open as though in surprise. He bent and pressed his lips softly to hers. "I've missed you. Missed you all day."

"Hello to you, too," she said huskily, lifting a hand to trail a light caress down his bare chest.

"You're not wearing my leis."

"I thought they'd wilt in the sun."

"I brought you a drink."

Their eyes spoke other words. Is it all right? Has anything changed? Can we keep on going from where we left off last night? They searched and found assurance that the sense of togetherness had not been shaken by the day apart.

"How did it go with Gail?" Sophie asked.

He grimaced. "Useless. It all rests with Randy now. Thank heaven he's coming tomorrow. If only I can persuade him to be reasonable, something might be salvaged."

He pulled up another lounger and sat on it, avidly running his eyes over her as she sipped the cocktail. "I looked for you as we were sailing past. And here you were like a siren of old, calling to me," he said, smiling into her eyes. "Fire-red hair and a hot yellow swimsuit singing out my name."

"You don't like my hair," Sophie said ruefully.

He laughed. "I'm beginning to adore your hair. It simply takes some getting used to. Besides, it's you."

Sophie wasn't sure what he meant by that but it sounded as though he no longer wanted to find any fault in her, that whatever encompassed her person or personality could only find favour with him. She wondered if that was truly so, or if the power of all the reaching out and the giving in the act of making love together simply erased all petty criticisms.

"What's on the menu tonight?" she asked. "Apart from me."

"Gail wants to meet you."

Sophie laughed outright. "You can't be serious! Gail wants to meet me as much as she wants a migraine headache."

"It's her decision."

She leaned over and took his hand. "Tell me this, Jason. Apart from your mother, every woman personally acquainted with you has been utterly bitchy to me. Why is that?"

"Because you're bold and bright and beautiful, and they can't compete with you," he rattled off as though it was perfectly obvious.

Sophie looked at him agape. "Is that what you think?"

He took her cocktail glass and set it down on the sand, then pulled her upright with him. "I think you're intelligent, vivacious and infinitely attractive. And I desire you madly."

He proved the latter claim by kissing her there and then in full view of anyone who cared to be looking. His desire was so obvious, and his kiss so stirring, that when his lips finally parted from hers, a sense of mutual and urgent accord started them walking down the beach towards their *faré*.

The sun was much lower in the sky when Sophie stirred from their bed to prepare for dinner with Gail Sullivan. She felt totally revitalised from Jason's exquisite lovemaking, and full of confidence for the evening ahead. Adrenalin zinged through her body as she showered and applied the appropriate war paint to meet the woman who had claimed most of Jason's attention for the past two days.

Gail Sullivan might have succumbed to curiosity about the new woman in Jason's life, but Sophie had no illusions about being offered an olive branch of peace and friendship. She hoped she was wrong, but all her female instincts warned her that Gail did not want to relinquish her claim on the man who had once been her lover.

Jason took over the bathroom as soon as Sophie emerged. She was already dressed and doing her nails when he reappeared. She whirled around for him to admire the jumpsuit she wore. The stretch fabric was a wild swirl of royal blue, lime green, hot pink and white. It hugged her body like a second skin, and the colourful swirls were cleverly designed to emphasise every feminine curve. It was definitely the most flamboyantly sexy outfit she had bought.

"Like it?" she asked.

"Stunning!" Jason said with satisfactory fervour.

"Stylish?"

"On you it is, Sophie. You've got the perfect figure to carry it off." He grinned. "But don't ever wear it to the office. I'd never get any work done."

"You'd only have eyes for me?"

He laughed. "It just about knocks my eyes out!"

Good! thought Sophie. She felt the need to go to dinner tonight with all guns firing. *Eat your heart out, Gail Sullivan,* she thought vehemently. *Jason is not yours for the picking anymore. He's mine!*

Sophie was even more pleased when Jason dressed to complement her outfit. His lime green sports shirt and white pants made her feel more firmly coupled with him. To cement them further, he linked her arm possessively with his as they strolled across the lawn to Gail's *faré.*

There was no doubt in Sophie's mind that Gail had gone all out for the kill, as well. She came swanning out in a swishy off-the-shoulder white gauze peasant dress that featured a festival of pastel ribbons and lace inserts. Ultra-feminine. Especially with her long mane of caramel hair teased into casual disarray. That alone must have taken her hours, Sophie thought, meeting the tigerish eyes of the other woman with limpid blue coolness.

Sophie was not about to be rattled by anything tonight. Jason might have been drawn to the more natural look in sophisticated women in the past, but despite that inclination, he had found Sophie not only desirable, but irresistible. There was no doubt in her mind that she was the woman in possession at the moment, and she was not averse to driving that point home to Gail. Besides, it might make the other woman reconsider her position with Randy. Which was what Jason wanted.

He smoothly performed a formal introduction, which was negotiated with sweet politeness by both women. Fortunately the path was wide enough for three abreast, and they strolled up to the hotel together. At Jason's suggestion they settled in the Matira Bar for a pre-dinner drink.

It was the perfect place for watching the sunset, which was utterly spectacular this evening. The cane armchairs with their brightly patterned cushions were set on swivel bases so they could be turned in any direction. It was an open-air room, and the bamboo railing and posts that supported the thickly plaited pandanus roof were minimal interruptions to the fabulous view.

The initial blaze of glory in the sky gradually faded to a soft pink, and the water shimmered with unbelievable light changes, from silvery aqua to a soft beige. Sophie commented on it as they sipped their drinks, saying she had never seen anything so intriguingly beautiful.

It was a harmless conversational remark, but Gail seized on it to fire off a patronising barb. "It must be very exciting for you to come here, Sophie," she said with an air of world-weariness, as though she had seen it all a thousand times before.

"Yes, it is," Sophie agreed with an appreciative smile.

"Youth is so enthusiastic," Gail said with sweet condescension. "When you've travelled far more extensively, as I have done, these things are seen in better proportion."

"Well, I hope I never lose my enthusiasm for beauty," Sophie replied just as sweetly. "I spent most of the past three years exploring Europe, and I loved every minute of it. Though I must admit I've only flown over the Pacific until now."

She paused to let that considerable range of worldly experience sink in, then fired a beneficial barb at Gail. "This beautiful island has opened my eyes to another world. And, I think, a much nicer one. It puts one back in touch with nature and the kind of values that we tend to overlook in our normal lives."

"Oh, really?" One finely arched eyebrow lifted sardonically. "What values are those?"

Sophie directed a broad smile at Jason. "Basic ones. Like a man and a woman finding out what they want with each other, without any outside pressures twisting up their minds."

Jason's eyes twinkled appreciation of her attempt to prepare the way for Randy's arrival, but Gail didn't like the private little intimacy between Jason and Sophie one bit. She made a pointed production of finishing her drink, then without waiting for them to do likewise, she stood up with an air of impatience.

"Shall we move into the dining room?"

They obliged her.

As soon as they were seated and handed menus, Gail opened up another attack. "What an original idea for you to dye your hair inferno red, Sophie!"

Sophie laughed. "Rather bright, isn't it? But Jason likes it, don't you, darling?"

"Yes. Very striking," he came in on cue.

"In fact, all the women in the office admired it so much, they went to my hairdresser to have theirs done the same," Sophie pressed on, determined to frustrate Gail's attempt to score a hit on her.

Gail looked at Jason incredulously. "You have an office full of red-haired women?"

"Yes," he said with a dry little smile. "Very becoming."

Gail's eyes glittered with the need to drive some wedge into their united front. "How do you find Jason to work for, Sophie?" she asked condescendingly.

Oh, no, you don't, Sophie thought with venom. *I'm more than his office assistant, so let's have no pre-*

tence about it! She studiously examined her hot-pink fingernails, which, surprisingly, did not clash with her hair, then wriggled them playfully as she addressed Gail's question, her eyes meeting the other woman's with a full blue blast of female gratification.

"Jason is a great lover," she stated decisively. "No question about that."

Jason's foot came into sharp contact with her shin under the table.

Undeterred, Sophie smiled fatuously at him. "Aren't you, darling?"

"I try," he said despairingly, recognising that the gloves were off and any hope of a friendly dinner had just disintegrated. "Now shall we concentrate on the menu and get our order together?" he suggested in a plea for a truce.

"Oh, what an original idea!" said Sophie brightly.

She scintillated through the whole meal while Gail sniped with all the ammunition she could muster. The more sour Gail's comments, the brighter Sophie's replies became. She gave the bubbliest performance of her life, loving the food, loving the wine and shooting a multitude of loving looks at Jason, who was most definitely caught between the devil and the deep blue sea.

He struggled valiantly to hold on to a neutral position throughout the ongoing battle. By the time they rose from the table, Gail had accepted defeat and had nothing at all to say as they walked back to their *farés*.

Sophie, however, had something to say when she and Jason reached the privacy of their living room.

"How could you have loved that woman?" she demanded. "She's so full of herself!"

There was a wash of pain across his face. "Don't, Sophie! You've had your pound of flesh tonight. Let it go."

His words stabbed straight to her heart. He might have supported her in front of Gail, but it seemed that his underlying loyalty lay with the other woman. It suddenly struck home to Sophie that she couldn't wipe out a relationship that had spanned many years. It had a shared solidity that gave it lasting power.

She had won the battle tonight but quite possibly she had lost the war in her blind need for supremacy in Jason's life. She should have been supporting him in his purpose instead of putting him into a no-win situation in having to support her against Gail.

"I'm sorry," she said stiffly. "I didn't set out to hurt you."

He took in her stricken face, winced at his own abruptness with her, then reached out and drew her into his embrace. Sophie stiffened against him. Couldn't help herself. She knew this was some decisive moment in their understanding of each other.

"I don't like to see any human being hurt, Sophie," he said quietly. He reached up and gently brushed his knuckles down her cheek. "Not you. Nor Gail. And the deeper pain is hers at the moment."

Guilt and justification warred through Sophie's mind. Would it have served Jason's purpose any better if she'd acted like a dumb punching bag for Gail? Didn't the other woman need a good jolt to set the situation to rights? Or was that too simple a viewpoint?

"You think what I did tonight was wrong?" she asked, needing to understand Jason's perception of Gail's behaviour.

He heaved a weary sigh. "No. You did nothing wrong, Sophie. It was all perfectly understandable. Gail started it. You finished it."

"But you'd rather I hadn't done that," she concluded from his tone of voice.

"A meeting place was lost," he said with regret that smote her heart.

She had forced him to choose, and he hadn't wanted to choose. Yet Gail was a stepping stone to the past, a past that had left Jason alone, bereft, miserable, discarded. Why should he want to hang on to it? He had said it was over for him. But perhaps it wasn't. Perhaps he wanted it to be over, but it wasn't.

"Do you still feel hurt by what happened between you and Gail?" Sophie asked, searching for some reassurance about her own position with him.

He lifted her chin with his hand, and his eyes burned into hers with a need that sought to obliterate everything else. "Whatever I feel," he said, "you assuage it when you're in my arms."

"You don't want to talk about it?"

"Would you want me to talk to some other person about what you and I have shared, Sophie?"

"No."

"Maybe some day—when the conditions are right— I can tell you everything. But not right now." His eyes begged her forbearance. "Can you accept that?"

"I have to, don't I?" she said, wondering if she was being an absolute fool. Yet as Jason's lips began to graze softly over hers, she knew that she wasn't prepared to give up on a future with him.

They made love. Not as wildly and passionately as before. Jason showed a caring and tenderness for her, as if reaching out for something they had not previously attained. Searching, adoring her body, looking into her eyes, questioning, and for long hours afterwards, holding her close as she snuggled languidly against him.

On the surface everything seemed perfect, but somehow, in some unknown way, Sophie felt that she had failed Jason. But she didn't know in what way, or how to put it right.

CHAPTER ELEVEN

RANDY ARRIVED ON SCHEDULE.

Jason and Sophie were left in no doubt about it. Gail marched down the beach to inform them in no uncertain terms. She also told Jason that if he thought he was a marriage counsellor, he was off his rocker. The marriage was finished, and he'd better have *her* best interests at heart when he got around to untangling the legal entanglements. *If* he could ever bring himself to lift his mind off other things.

This last was said with a venomous glare at Sophie, who was languidly stretched out on a lounger while Jason smoothed block-out lotion over her back.

"I do have your best interests at heart, Gail," he answered her quietly. "I'm sorry you don't see it that way. If you'd like to join us and talk about it, you're very welcome."

She muttered something that sounded like, "In a pig's ear!" and tramped off again.

Randy ambled down five minutes later, looking exactly like the soap opera hero he played on television. His physique was every bit as trim, taut and terrific as it was on screen. His handsome face had a rakish look, accentuated by thickly lashed green eyes, wickedly arched eyebrows and the longish blonde hair that was artfully sun-streaked to go with his image.

"You owe me a drink, Jason," he started accusingly. "You bring me all the way to Bora Bora and the first thing I find is my wife next door to me. Paradise ruined!"

"I'm sure I can get something to anaesthetise the pain, Randy."

"You do that. And I'll take over oiling the body beautiful for you," he said with a leer at Sophie.

"Uh-uh! Hands off, my friend. This lady is mine," Jason warned in a tone that raised Randy's eyebrows.

"You're serious?"

"Never more so."

Randy broke into a delighted chuckle. "No wonder Gail's spitting chips!" He rubbed his hands together in glee. "I love it, love it, love it! No more Old Faithful! Introduce me to your fabulous floozy, Jason."

"Sophie is not a—"

"Gail's word, old chap. Sophie is fine by me. Sophie is a beautiful name. Sophie, I adore you. Call me Randy," he burbled, flirting outrageously with his eyes.

Jason heaved an exasperated sigh. "I'll get us some drinks." He dropped a kiss on Sophie's shoulder. "A Chi Chi for you?"

"Yes, please."

As Jason set off for the bar, Randy pulled another lounger into place beside theirs. He sat on it and grinned at Sophie, whose spirits had lifted immeasurably at Jason's show of possessiveness towards her. She desperately hoped it hadn't been an act for Randy's benefit.

"Why did you call Jason Old Faithful?" she asked, still troubled by what she perceived as too long a hangover from his relationship with Gail.

Randy's grin grew wider. "Gail thought she had him on a string because he's never married. Pure ego on her part. Which I'm glad to see stung. But let's not talk about Jason. Nor the thorn in my side that I had the misfortune to marry. Let's talk about you."

He rolled out the last sentence in his famous sexy voice, and Sophie couldn't help laughing at it. "Randy, all your female co-stars might fall for that line, but I'm immune."

"The camera would love you, Sophie," he said, undeterred by her negative response. "Dump Jason, come with me, and I'll get you a part in the show."

"You're still a married man," she reminded him.

"Not for much longer. I'll soon be footloose and fancy-free." He swung his legs onto the lounger and stretched out with an exaggerated sigh of contentment. "What I need is a woman who'll accept me as I am. Now tell me, Sophie—" his green eyes swam with eloquent appeal "—is that too much to ask?"

Sophie grinned. "Depends on how many warts you have."

"Do you see any?" he demanded.

"Are you claiming to be perfect?"

He bantered on, demonstrating the good-humoured charm that had won the hearts of television viewers all over Australia. Until recently, he and Gail were the perfectly paired lovers on the long-running soap opera that dominated the ratings. Their real-life wedding had been paralleled in the show, to the viewers' delighted approval, but no-one had expected or wanted their fictional marital problems to come true.

Jason returned with the drinks and Sophie made room on her lounger for him to sit beside her. He smiled at her as she snuggled around him, the warm memory of other intimacies in his eyes.

"Boy, oh boy!" Randy sighed. "I think I'll have to chat up one of the lovely Polynesians. Looking at you two is enough to stir the blood."

"You could make up with your wife, Randy," Jason dryly pointed out.

"Not in a million years," came the emphatic reply. Randy drank the beer Jason had brought him as though he needed to take some nasty taste out of his mouth. Then he shot a hard, derisive look at the man who had stood beside him on his wedding day. "If that's what's on your mind, forget it. No deal. No nothing. I am here strictly for fun and forgetfulness."

"Which you'll undoubtedly find at the bottom of your usual bottle," Gail's voice sliced in with a strong dash of vinegar.

They all looked up as she sauntered across the sand from the lawn behind them. She wore a skimpy white bikini that displayed a body that was the female counterpart of Randy's, trim and taut and terrific. Her long hair was wound into a loose knot on top of her head. She carried a beach towel and a white and gold pareu, and flashed them a smile that had all the threat of a piranha on the prowl.

"What the hell do you think you're doing?" Randy growled as she laid the towel on Jason's lounger.

"Joining the party. Jason said I was welcome to."

"What happened to catching the first flight out of Bora Bora?" Randy demanded fiercely.

She glared at him with tigerish eyes. "You can do that, Randy. I was here first. Why should I let you spoil my vacation?"

"If you think I'm going to leave this paradise on your account, you can think again. I'm staying right here in the accommodation I've paid for," he stated belligerently.

"And I'm staying in mine," Gail retorted.

As she sat down, Randy stood up.

"I'm going to the bar."

Gail's eyes glittered with malicious intent. "Let's all go to the bar. It's such a thirsty morning, isn't it?"

That set the pattern of the day. If Gail wasn't taunting Randy about some failing in personality or character, he was letting her know, with devastating and diabolical charm, where she fell short of perfection. The knives were out with a vengeance, and Sophie mentally marked it down as the Day of a Thousand Cuts.

Jason and Sophie served two purposes. They provided a neutral area where Randy and Gail could retreat to safety from the blood-letting in their guerilla warfare. They also provided an audience, which both the antagonists relished. However, the strain of being a buffer zone was certainly telling on Jason by the time they headed for their *farés* to refresh themselves before another bout over dinner.

"This idea of setting them both on an island isn't going to work, Sophie," he said wearily.

"They're together, aren't they?" Sophie pointed out. "And talking to each other."

Jason rolled his eyes. "Do you call that talking? Both of them are beyond reason!"

"But they can't leave each other alone. And since when did love have anything to do with reason?"

"Love!" Jason scoffed. "They *hate* each other."

"Isn't hate the other side of love?"

Jason shot her a derisive look. "You're a romantic, Sophie."

"I'm also a realist," she said flatly.

Her tone of voice must have jarred something in Jason's mind. He said nothing while they washed the sand from their feet under the tap by the porch, but once inside the privacy of their living room he turned to her with sharply questioning eyes.

"What's on your mind, Sophie? Give me your advice."

The fears and doubts that had been raised last night demanded expression. "I think you're too mixed up in this situation to see straight," she blurted out.

"What should I be seeing?"

Her eyes held his in direct and unwavering challenge. "I know you didn't like what I did with Gail last night, but it directed her undivided attention to Randy today because she knew you were a lost cause."

"She already knew that," Jason said impatiently.

"Did she? When you danced attendance on her at her every demand? When you have, at the very least, a caring tenderness for her?"

He frowned, clearly discomfited by Sophie's critical appraisal of his behaviour.

"You told me on the plane that Gail had to be convinced you were not available to her," she reminded him. "You didn't do that, Jason. I did. And whatever you feel for her, if you're genuine in wanting her and Randy's marriage mended, I didn't do any damage to that purpose last night."

His eyes held a guarded reserve as he digested her remarks. Having opened the floodgates on her reservations about his responses to the situation, Sophie poured out the rest of her feelings.

"I asked Randy this morning why he called you Old Faithful. He said Gail thought she had you on a string because you'd never married."

"She didn't," Jason said tersely.

"Neither she nor Randy knew that. Randy was delighted that Gail could no longer use you against him. Which, to me, was very revealing."

Again Jason frowned, mulling over what she was saying.

"Sometimes you have to be cruelly honest to be kind," she said quietly. "Maybe that doesn't sit well with you where Gail is concerned, but in cutting the string last night, the field is now clear for Gail and Randy to get back together again. If that's what you want," she added uncertainly.

"Of course it's what I want," he snapped. "But I can't see it happening on today's showing. And to suggest that I was the only bone of contention between them is ridiculous!"

"Don't you think this whole thing is about being insecure with each other? Randy flirting with his costars? Gail holding you up to him as a threat?"

"God knows!" He shook his head. "All I know is the whole thing's beyond reason."

To Sophie's mind, Jason was protesting too much. It was as though he didn't want to hear what she was saying. It made her feel she didn't know where she fitted into the picture with him. She wasn't sure if Jason knew what the picture was anymore. The lines he had drawn were obscured by his reaction to last night's scene with Gail. Even more obscured by his negative view of today's events.

"Well, I guess I'm only here to provide you with fun and forgetfulness," she said self-mockingly, recalling Randy's words of this morning.

Jason was visibly jolted out of his introspection. "Don't be absurd, Sophie! You know you're necessary to the whole scheme."

Her eyes derided his claim. "Which scheme is that, Jason? The one where having me assuages what you feel for Gail?"

He looked appalled. "What I feel with you has nothing to do with Gail."

"I'm only repeating what you said last night," she said flatly.

Anguish twisted across his face. "You've misinterpreted what I meant. It's not like that, Sophie."

He came forward to wrap her in his arms. She did not resist, but she rested her hands on his chest, reluctant to be swept into a physical communication. "What is it like?" she asked, searching his eyes for the truth.

He did not try to evade the issue. "There are many shades of grey between black and white, Sophie," he said softly. "Perhaps I am too involved in the situation with Gail and Randy to see it clearly, but I know I'm not seeking forgetfulness with you. I want what we have together. It's something apart from this mess. Something new and beautiful."

Sophie took considerable encouragement from these words, and when he tenderly cupped her face in his hands and kissed her as though he truly cherished what he had found with her, she couldn't help responding with all her heart.

I have to trust what I feel with him, she thought, winding her arms around his neck and holding on tight. *It couldn't feel this right between us if Gail still held his heart. He must be mixed up in his mind about her.*

Sophie clung to that belief throughout the evening they spent with Gail and Randy. It would have been a magical evening, but for the intrusive disharmony of the feuding couple and Jason's tense awareness of his failure in the role of peace-maker. A full moon beamed its benevolence on the Tahitian barbecue that was held on the beach, and a local group of Polynesian singers and dancers provided spectacular entertainment. The dance group, in particular, put a temporary halt to the feuding between Gail and Randy.

To the mood-setting beat of wooden drums, torches were set aflame and held by a line of dancers along the water's edge. Then, sweeping fast around the point, came the traditional Tahitian sailing canoe bringing more dancers, some balancing on the outrigger with their torches aloft. It was a stunning beginning to a dance program that was totally mesmerising in its sinuous grace, its wildly primitive energy and its erotic insinuations.

Towards the end of the show, some of the hotel guests were invited to partner the Polynesian dancers. Gail instantly leapt up from her seat to offer herself to the most skilled of the male performers, whereupon Randy made a point of claiming the attention of the most beautiful female performer. Under the persuasive tuition and good-humoured encouragement of the dancers, Gail was soon shaking her hips in a highly suggestive and provocative manner, and Randy countered her triumph by mastering the rapid knee movement the men used to fasten attention on their powerful thighs.

When other guests gave up trying to copy the highly skilled movements, the male dancers gathered in a circle around Gail, egging her on, and Randy received the same accolade from the female dancers, much to the amusement and applause of the spectators. Neither Gail nor Randy needed anyone else to drive them into being star performers. It was the battle of the sexes with a vengeance, and the competition to match or surpass each other as stars in the eyes of others was fast and furious.

When the wild beat of the drums finally ceased, the dancers adorned them with many leis and escorted them to their seats.

"That gives me a new lease on life," Randy crowed, his face sparkling with triumph and pleasure.

Gail gave him a smug smile. "Yes," she agreed. "I now see what I've been missing out on."

"If you'd put as much energy into our sex life as you put into that dance, my dear, you wouldn't have missed out on anything," Randy drawled.

"With a man worn out from spending his energy elsewhere?" Gail scoffed.

"Ah, yes, of course." Randy smiled derisively. "The fantasy infidelities to excuse your lack of interest."

"That hardly needs excusing, with you hitting the bottle every night."

"A friendly haze in the mind tends to diminish the power of a ghost in the bed."

Jason's fingers tightened around Sophie's hand, almost crushing her. He rose to his feet, drawing her with him. "If you'll excuse us, Sophie and I want an early night."

"You have my blessings, old chap," Randy drawled. "With a woman like Sophie to warm the cockles of your heart, who wouldn't want an early night?"

For once, Gail had no ready rejoinder. She stared out to sea, ignoring Sophie's and Jason's departure. Randy's shaft about a ghost in the bed was clearly a double-edged sword. Not only had it cut down any counter offensive from Gail, but it had driven Jason into fast retreat from the battlefield. Sophie was well aware of his intense inner turmoil as they walked down the beach to their *faré*. He was grimly silent but his fingers kept dragging over the skin of her hand in constant agitation.

Sophie had no doubt whatsoever about who the ghost in the bed was. Jason was Gail's former lover, and it was now obvious that somewhere along the line, she regretted having rejected him to marry Randy. Had possibly taunted Randy by telling him Jason was a better lover. Which would be death to any marriage.

However, that was not Sophie's problem. Jason's reaction to that revelation was her problem. Was he wishing he had left the door open for Gail to come back to him? As much as it pained her, Sophie felt she had to find out.

"Have you given up on trying to persuade Gail and Randy to get back together?" she asked.

He heaved a deep sigh. "Maybe it's better for them to cut their losses than to try patching up something that's not working. What they're doing to each other... it's too destructive," he said sadly.

"So you think they might be better off apart?"

"I hate seeing a marriage break up, but—" he shook his head "—there's no meeting ground."

"Do you mind if I try?" Sophie pressed, anxious to get rid of the potential risk to her future with Jason. "I know we agreed that you'd have four days working your scheme your way, and it's only been three so far, but if you're ready to give up now, I'd like to have a try."

He gave her a wry smile. "Ever the optimist, Sophie?"

"Do you want me to try or not, Jason?" she quietly challenged, her heart tightening at his evasion of her offer.

He shrugged. "I doubt it will do any good, but you're welcome to try."

Relief bubbled through her. It no longer mattered to her if he was assuaging other feelings in her arms, as long as he was hers. And stayed hers.

"Well, I'll give it my best shot," she said brightly. "Of course, the results might be cosmic, so you'd better make wild and passionate love to me tonight."

It teased a laugh out of him. "Live for now, because tomorrow might be blown apart?"

"You have some argument against that?"

He released her hand and tucked her close to him. "Not me! You've been generating cosmic results ever since you walked into my life." He gave her an appreciative smile. "It will be no hardship to meet your requirements."

By the time Sophie finally snuggled down to go to sleep, she was satisfied that Jason was no longer thinking of Gail. Or Randy. Or anyone. He was too exhausted to think at all. And he wore a contented look on his face.

How she was going to resolve the conflict between Gail and Randy Sophie had no idea, but it had to be done somehow. She genuinely believed that they did care about each other underneath the festering wounds to their pride. Besides, only by getting them back together again could she feel secure about a long and lasting future with Jason.

CHAPTER TWELVE

JASON WAS STILL heavily asleep when Sophie woke the next morning. She let him stay that way. The last thing she needed was to have him tired and bad-tempered. Besides, if Jason remained out of action for a while, it gave her a completely free hand to try her luck at sorting out Gail and Randy, should the warring couple present an opportunity.

She had little choice but to play by ear. Whatever the outcome, Sophie had no illusions that she was going to be covered with acclaim or have all ribbons flying for her wonderful perspicacity. Gail disliked her too intensely for that to occur, and since Gail and Randy were both beyond reason, sweetness and light were not going to work. Sophie figured her only recourse was shock tactics, but what or how or when were very much up in the air.

She was late for breakfast. All the smaller tables around the lower deck of the restaurant were occupied, so she sat at a table for four on the higher level. Randy was even later. Sophie had already ordered but he made a beeline for her table.

Sophie didn't believe for one second that she exerted any real power of attraction over Randy. From the moment Gail had shown antagonism towards Jason's woman, Sophie was a mandatory target for flirtation. Randy was simply hamming up an interest, his mind and heart bent on hitting back at Gail for throwing Jason in his face.

It undoubtedly riled Gail all the more because Sophie was such a different physical type to herself, and having both her former lover and her husband apparently besotted by Sophie's charms was a double whammy to her ego.

Despite Randy's vengeful purpose, Sophie figured that his determination to put on a show of finding her irresistibly attractive should be encouraged for the time being. It might work to her advantage in the tricky task of getting him and Gail back together again. Wherever Randy was, Gail was sure to turn up sooner or later.

"How are you this morning?" she asked, giving him a bright welcoming smile.

"Dreadful!" he said. "The pain! The hurt! I suffer! I need your soothing hands to heal me, Sophie."

"Try some tomato juice and coffee to start with," she advised kindly.

One of the Polynesian waitresses came to take his order. She was still writing it down when Gail swept into the restaurant and claimed the chair beside Randy.

"Good morning!" she trilled.

Randy clasped his head and groaned.

"Good morning," Sophie returned politely.

Gail rattled off her breakfast order to the waitress, then stabbed a jaundiced look at Sophie. "Lost your lover along the way?"

"Jason is dead tired. I left him sleeping."

Randy heaved a theatrical sigh. "Lucky Jason! Sleeping the sleep of a satisfied man. You're all woman, Sophie."

"And so very obvious about it," Gail sneered. "I hope you don't imagine that Jason would ever consider you wife material."

"Take no notice of her, Sophie," Randy chimed in. "Jason is as smitten as any man in love could be. And why not? You're a jewel of womanhood."

"He won't marry her," Gail grated.

"Like to have a little wager on that, my sweet?" Randy challenged mockingly.

Sophie saw her chance and grabbed it. She gave a tinkling laugh. "Both of you are crazy. Even if Jason begged me on bended knee, I'm certainly not going to marry him. Marriage is for the birds! Look what it did to you two!"

Her eyes swept them both with amused derision before dropping to her plate. She busied herself spreading some strawberry conserve over a piece of toast, then blithely bit into it, as though she were completely at peace with her world.

"Just what do you mean by that?" Gail demanded, her tigerish eyes flashing resentment at Sophie's judgement of them. "I am perfectly fine, thank you."

"Well, I'd hate to see you on your bad days, Gail," Sophie observed.

"Marriage is a growing experience!" Randy declared with dry irony..

"Sure! It grows right into the divorce court," Sophie lightly mocked. "There you were, the perfect lovers, with what seemed to the world a perfect match for marriage. People looked up to you as an ideal of how love should turn out." She wrinkled her nose. "Some ideal, when it degenerates into a cat and dog fight! If you two couldn't make marriage work, what chance have the rest of us?"

"Nobody should make idols of other people," Gail snapped.

"I refuse to be responsible for how others think or live," Randy drawled with supreme world-weariness.

"Oh, don't get me wrong!" Sophie said with a silky smile. "I'm grateful to both of you. You've proved to me that even the shiniest love doesn't last for long. The best thing to do is enjoy it while everything's great, then skip off when the going gets tough. That way you stay ahead of the game."

Randy looked vexed at Sophie's open scorn for the breakdown of his marriage. It was spoiling his game with her.

Gail looked grimly furious.

Sophie ate another bite of toast, then leaned forward earnestly. "By being such spectacular losers, you've taught me how not to end up a loser. You've both been a great example of what can happen if you tie yourself up with commitments."

"I am never a loser, Sophie," Randy insisted, clearly disliking her blunt interpretation of his position.

"What about the business contracts you're busting up?" Sophie reminded him. "As Jason's assistant, I've seen your joint file. You're both going to lose a packet when the divorce goes through. Not to mention the division of the domiciles and the—"

"That's *our* business!" Gail almost spit in outrage.

"Soon to be all public, isn't it?" Sophie retorted. "Dirty linen everywhere. Disgusting, really. I'm going to keep all my affairs private."

"Does Jason know that you regard what you're having with him as a passing affair?" Randy asked, his eyes narrowing in some private speculation.

"Hmm..." Sophie cocked her head consideringly. "I think I'd call it a stylish affair. A *very* stylish affair. I've never had a lover who bought me such lovely clothes before."

"He went so far as to buy you clothes?" Gail gasped.

"That's really serious for him," Randy muttered. "You didn't answer my question, Sophie. Is Jason aware of this attitude of yours?"

Sophie shrugged. "What difference does it make? We're having a super time together." She gave Gail a sly look. "I can understand about the ghost in the bed. Jason is *great* between the sheets."

Gail went bright red. "Nowhere near as great as Randy!" she snarled. "Even dead drunk, Randy is a better lover than Jason ever was! I only baited Randy with that to pay him back for his rotten flirting."

"Why, Gail!" Randy beamed at her.

"Don't get tickets on yourself! There are other fish in the sea!" She nodded at Sophie. "I told you she was a floozy, Randy."

"Better a floozy than a dumped wife," Sophie said blithely.

"Now hang on a minute!" Randy protested. "I didn't dump Gail. She walked out on me."

"Well, more fool her if you're such a fantastic lover." Sophie batted her eyelashes at him. "Look me up when you're footloose and fancy-free, Randy. This thing I've got going with Jason will probably be wearing thin by then."

"You're nothing but a disgusting little man-eater," Gail cried in towering contempt.

Sophie raised her eyebrows. "On the contrary, you're the one tearing Randy apart. At least I give a man what he wants." She smiled at Randy. "You can count on me to make you feel whole again."

"I think I'd rather give the job to someone with a heart," he said, his pretend interest in her considerably cooled. "What I once had with my wife appeals more."

Sophie looked at him pityingly. "Well, if you want to fool yourself with dreams..."

"It was not a dream!" Gail replied angrily.

"Best part of my life," Randy admitted with wry regret.

"Mine, too," Gail said.

Sophie pushed back her chair and rose to her feet, shaking her head at both of them. "Who do you think you're kidding? If that was the best, why did you botch it up? If you'll excuse me, I'm off to buy some souvenirs."

She paused to give them a condescending smile. "Once you're divorced you'll be able to live like me. Have three lovers at any time. One to take you to lovely places like this. One to let your hair down with. And one to provide a steady support to fall back on. That way you can always keep your joie de vivre."

"A three-timing gold-digger!" Gail cried. "You're amoral, immoral and despicable!"

"Ah! But I have only good memories," Sophie pointed out triumphantly.

"A user," Randy muttered, his eyes contemptuously dismissing any further use of her in his wife-baiting.

Sophie smiled brightly at him. "I always give fair value, Randy, and I wouldn't give you any problem getting rid of me when things turn sour." She slanted a pointed look at Gail. "No nasty comebacks in a law court for the media to gobble up with glee."

She had certainly provoked at least one mutual feeling between them. They both glared at her with open hostility.

Sophie stepped around the table and gave Randy's shoulder a light squeeze. "Remind me to give you my address before Jason and I fly out. And believe me, I never take a man down when it's over. Live for the day. That's my motto."

The Polynesian waitress arrived with Gail's and Randy's breakfast orders. Sophie wriggled her fingers at them in a farewell salute and made off while the going was good. She felt quite satisfied that she had hit them with some fine left and right jabs. The silence she left behind her definitely had a punch-drunk quality. Of course, they could come out of it slugging at each other again, but they showed every indication of forming a new accord, if only against her.

Sophie strolled down the road to the Pofai Shoppe, then on to the Moana Art Gallery-Boutique, looking for and buying little gifts for all the women on Jason's staff. Their support of her deserved some friendly recognition. She also had to buy something really special for Mia, finally deciding on a dramatic shell necklace.

By the time she returned to the *faré* with her purchases, Jason was awake and under the shower. Sophie opened the bathroom door and admired his sleekly muscled body until he turned his back to the spray of water and saw her.

"Hi!" she said with a cheeky grin. "Feeling more rested and ready to join the fray again?"

"I missed you." He turned off the taps and grabbed a towel. "Why didn't you wake me? Most of the morning's gone."

"Don't worry. Nothing's lost. I saw Gail and Randy at breakfast and did my bit to drive them back together."

"Sophie—" he looked alarmed "—what have you done?"

"Set the cat amongst the pigeons," she replied airily. "Hit them with a few home truths. And left them with not much of an appetite for biting into each other. I hope."

He dried himself very briskly. "What's going to happen?" he demanded.

"Jason, when you set off an explosion, the only thing you can do is stand back and wait to see where the pieces fall."

He groaned. "Well, I don't suppose it can be any worse than what it was yesterday."

"That's the spirit," Sophie encouraged. "I've been shopping, as well. Very hot outside. If we go up to the Pofai Bar I can have a drink and you can get something to eat."

"And Randy will probably be there, drowning his sorrows," Jason muttered, hurling the towel aside. He heaved a deep sigh, gave Sophie a rueful smile, then drew her into his arms and spent a few minutes kissing her in little nibbles. "Maybe all I want to eat is you," he murmured.

Sophie wound a few of his chest hairs around her index finger. "Jason . . ."

"Mmm?"

"You do remember our purpose in coming here?"

"Mmm."

"You really want Gail and Randy back together again?"

"Mmm."

"Well, if you hear a few bad things about me, that won't make any difference to what you feel with me, will it?"

He cupped her face and looked deeply into her eyes. "Sophie, nothing at all could shake what you make me feel," he said with conviction, then touched the fiery profusion of her red curls with indulgent affection. "I'm getting used to your brand of dynamite."

She slid her hands over his shoulders and tilted her head back, giving him an inviting smile. "Do you want to go and have breakfast, or would you prefer—"

"I prefer," he said huskily.

WHEN THEY WENT up to the Pofai Bar for lunch, Gail and Randy were nowhere to be seen. Sophie and Jason spent a leisurely couple of hours there without any interruption from the warring couple.

"Did you hit them so hard they've run for cover?" Jason asked Sophie.

She shrugged. "Let's forget them and enjoy the peace while it lasts."

They spent an idyllic afternoon. Sophie saved a few crusts of bread from their lunch and they waded out to the large coral outcrop where a swarm of brilliantly coloured tropical fish made their home. It was fun dropping crumbs in the water and watching the incredible speed of the fish darting out for food. Some even nibbled at Sophie's fingers for more.

Then Jason decided to try his hand at paddling one of the canoes that were available for the guests' use, and he took Sophie well out into the lagoon, proving very skilful at manoeuvring the small craft. It was lovely to leave other people's problems behind and immerse themselves in sharing the pleasure of the beauty around them.

"I don't think I've ever felt more at peace," Jason remarked, his eyes soft and shiny with happiness. "You're a joy to be with, Sophie."

She laughed, bubbling with her own happiness. "It's quite a change, isn't it?" she replied. "No business rules. No schemes. Just you and me and all this!"

"Paradise found," he said with an appreciative smile. "I've been looking for it for a long time."

Sophie's heart turned over at the possessive way his gaze swept over her. *It is right,* she thought exultantly. *We are truly right together. He feels it, too.*

The feeling grew stronger and more certain as they filled all the hours of that day with a special sense of togetherness. The heady romance of a sunset cruise was followed by a delightful dinner at Bloody Mary's Hotel, a famed place from the movie *South Pacific.*

They sat on the cutoff trunks of coconut trees, sipped freshly crushed pineapple juice, ate the local food from the cooking pit and pretended they were castaways from the rest of the world.

When they returned to their hotel, Jason suggested a moonlight swim, and that was right, too, floating under the stars, revelling in a sense of total freedom with each other, a mingling of bodies and souls in a harmonious rhythm of life. They did not speak of love, yet it was in each look and touch, and when they finally sought the intimate privacy of their *faré* they made love long into the night.

The pieces from Sophie's explosion commenced landing the next morning. Jason and Sophie were lazing on the beach when they noticed the approach of the couple who had received the brunt of yesterday's blast. Having been lost for twenty-four hours, their reappearance in the form of a grim-faced united front bounced a few other things up in the air.

Like Sophie's future with Jason.

"They're holding hands!" Jason said in shock, turning incredulous eyes to Sophie. "How on earth did you achieve that?"

"Do you trust me, Jason?" she asked as calmly as she could.

"Yes, of course. Haven't I given you my complete confidence?"

Not quite, Sophie thought. There was still the touchy matter about his feelings for Gail, which he had left unanswered. "I think it's very important to trust what you feel about another person," she said emphatically. "So please don't let anything Gail and Randy say change how you feel about me. Okay?"

He frowned. "What do you mean?"

Sophie sighed in resignation. "You'll soon find out."

The omens were not good when Gail and Randy elected to disdain acknowledging Sophie's presence by either word or look. They came to a halt beside Jason's lounger, and Randy addressed him in solemn tones.

"Gail and I wish to speak to you, Jason. Alone and in private," he said with pointed emphasis.

"We thought my *faré* would be the best place," Gail put in.

"You've come to some agreement?" Jason queried, still finding it difficult to believe.

"Gail and I are in complete agreement on everything," Randy declared. "If you'll come with us, there are a few things we want to settle with you personally, Jason."

"Because you've been a good friend to both Randy and me," Gail said feelingly.

"And we care about you," Randy backed up.

Jason slowly swung his legs off the lounger, stood up and shot a puzzled look of appeal at Sophie. "Wait here for me?"

"You might be some time, Jason," she replied with a wry little smile. "If I'm not here or swimming, I'll be in our *faré*."

If there was going to be any problem between them, Sophie didn't want Gail and Randy witnessing it. Jason nodded, flashed her one last smile, then went off to reseal the friendship being offered to him.

CHAPTER THIRTEEN

JASON WAS IN CONFERENCE with Randy and Gail for a long time. Sophie idled away an hour in the lagoon, not so much swimming as enjoying the lulling swell and ebb of the soft wavelets that kept her body light and buoyant. Her mind kept reciting there was no point in worrying about what was going on, but her heart defied all acts of will and persisted in twisting itself into uncertain little knots.

She felt a surge of relief when she saw Jason emerge from the private talk unaccompanied by the others. However, he did not so much as sweep a quick glance over the beach or the lagoon. He headed straight up the path to the hotel administration centre, looking like a man on a purposeful mission.

Business? Sophie wondered. Perhaps Jason had to do some unwrangling for the Sullivans if their marriage was back on the road. Nevertheless, she couldn't help thinking it was a bad sign that Jason hadn't looked for her.

She waded out of the lagoon, observing that Randy and Gail were still closeted together in private, possibly awaiting Jason's return. Having collected the various articles she and Jason had taken down to the beach, Sophie went to their *faré* to get cleaned up for lunch. She was under the shower when she heard the front door bang shut. The careless noise was followed by other sounds of things being shifted around in an angry and impatient manner.

Sophie turned off the taps, wrapped herself in a large bath towel and with her heart thumping in fast agitation went to investigate the cause of the disturbance. She found Jason hurling clothes into his suitcase, which lay open on the bed.

"Going somewhere?" she asked, confronting the obvious issue first.

He wheeled on her, his face as grim as death, his silvery grey eyes glittering with barely controlled anger. "Yes," he snapped. "We're going home. The flights have been booked and I've organised for a boat to take us to the airport. You have an hour to get ready. If you've finished with the bathroom, I'll have my shower now."

Sophie propped herself in the doorway to the dressing room, defying his overbearing manner. "I'm not going!" she said.

"What?"

His face contorted with outrage. Clearly he was not used to being defied. Sophie, however, saw no other course but to take the bull by the horns and give it a good shake.

"You're acting like a bad-tempered schoolboy who's lost his toffee apple. The least you can do is tell me if I pulled off mission impossible for you."

"The laurels are all yours," he said sarcastically.

Jason's stormy mood robbed Sophie of any sense of triumph. "So what's the problem, Jason? Did you realise too late that you wanted Gail back after all?"

"Why would I want Gail?" he thundered.

"You did have a long affair with her," Sophie prodded.

"That doesn't mean I want her back."

"You could have fooled me," Sophie said offhandedly.

"Then I'll spell it out to you," he snarled, fuming with frustration. "It was never a serious affair. Not on my side. And I didn't know it was on her side until she brought up marriage. We had separate careers. Led separate lives. When we connected, it was good, but I never saw us as settling into a permanent future together. I was sorry that she did. Sorry that I hurt her—"

"You mean *you* broke it off with Gail before she married Randy?"

"Haven't I just told you that?"

"It wasn't *she* who rejected you?" Sophie pressed.

Jason hissed impatiently. "Have some sense, Sophie! I agreed to support that story for Gail's sake. So her image wouldn't be hurt in her career. There wouldn't have been a problem if she'd rejected me, would there?"

That was purely dependent on one's point of view, thought Sophie. To make doubly sure of what Jason meant, she asked, "Then you don't mind that she and Randy have resumed wedded bliss?"

"For God's sake! That was what this trip was all about." He glowered at her. "At least now I don't have to feel guilty about Gail any more."

"That was all you felt? Guilt?"

He grimaced. "And compassion for the hurt she'd suffered from both me and Randy. I was never sure she hadn't married Randy on the rebound. When the marriage went wrong, it seemed that I might be responsible. It was a hell of a position to be in."

"You can't blame yourself for what others choose to do with their lives," Sophie soothed, delighted that Gail could now be painted out of the picture of Jason's love life.

"That's easier said than done," he muttered. "Since Gail, I've been a damned sight more careful about choosing my associations with women—"

Which accounted for the likes of Evonne Carstairs, Sophie deduced.

"Until you came along," Jason finished with seething bitterness.

"Something wrong with me?" she asked.

His eyes flared with bolts of turbulent lightning. "How many lovers have you got?" he demanded.

So this was the crux of all the bad temper! Sophie's heart untwisted itself and swelled with satisfaction. Jealousy. Possession punctured by tales from her brilliant invention.

The urge to reassure him was dampened by the thought that he should have trusted her. She had asked him to, and he should have known better than to believe what she'd told Gail and Randy in his commercial interests. She was not about to get on her knees to grovel for forgiveness about something she hadn't done. Let him take the consequences of his impaired judgement! If he'd been more open about Gail in the first place, Sophie would not have felt compelled to do what she'd done to get Gail safely tied up with Randy again.

"Answer me, Sophie!" he seethed. "How many men have you got on a string?"

"Enough to keep me satisfied," she said airily.

He breathed in and out so heavily that steam seemed to come out of his nostrils. "Gail and Randy said you advocate three at a time."

"Well," said Sophie, "it's a small enough number to keep track of them, but large enough to make life interesting."

"You're going to have to get rid of two of them!" he thundered.

"That won't be too difficult," she said.

"Good! Because you're going to do it the moment we get home. I might have rocks in my head for brains but that's the way it has to be."

Sophie raised her eyebrows. "Do I understand you want exclusive rights with me?"

"You'd better believe it," he threatened.

A marvellous feeling of security swept through Sophie. Her uncertainties about Jason's feelings for her were finally laid to rest. She was free of any further torment on that score. Which meant she could deal from a position of strength.

"I don't take very kindly to being ordered around, Jason," she told him mildly. "It's one thing as my boss. That's fair enough. But if you want to be my one and only lover..."

He reined in his feelings and adopted the face of stern authority. "The job we came to do is done, Sophie. It's best if we leave now and let Randy and Gail get on with their second honeymoon without any distraction from us. I'm telling you that as your boss," he said curtly.

"Fine. But that does give us some free days, doesn't it?" Sophie argued. "And you must admit I've been a very effective assistant in helping to get the result you wanted. I understand that it's prudent to leave Bora Bora right now, but we don't have to fly straight home to Australia, do we?"

He heaved a deep sigh. "What's on your mind, Sophie?"

"Well, maybe I need some convincing that you're the only lover I want, Jason. You're not being very nice to me at the moment. You're all demand. No asking me what I'd like. That doesn't feel right to me."

"Dammit, Sophie!" he cried in exasperation. "We *are* right together! And there's no room for anyone else!" To prove it, he swept her into his arms and kissed any other possible thought out of her head. "We can stop in Tahiti, if you want," he said gruffly. "But we've got to get moving now."

Sophie was so dazzled by Jason's possessive passion for her she couldn't resist finding out how far it extended. Particularly since she had been tearing herself up about having any kind of future with him.

True to his word, Jason rebooked their flight, and they stayed the extra two days at the Beachcomber Parkroyal Hotel on the outskirts of Papeete. He also made a crusade of asking Sophie what she would like to do and fulfilling her every wish. Which wasn't really difficult. Basically it was time with him that Sophie wanted, time to affirm and consolidate what they felt for each other.

They spent a wonderful day wandering around Papeete. The influence of French settlement was very much in evidence with its distinctive style of European sophistication, yet overall, the colour and vivacity of Polynesian life held sway. Simply to sit at the sidewalk cafés and watch the stream of people and traffic was a delight to Sophie, and Jason happily shared her mood.

He took pleasure in buying her almost anything and everything she admired, from a Tahiti tiare lei with its glorious gardenia scent to an exquisite necklace of black pearls. There was a very determined glint of possessiveness in his eyes as he fastened that around her neck and insisted she wear it out of the boutique.

"You're spoiling me rotten," she teased, her own eyes lit with dancing pleasure.

"I have this vision of making love to you with those pearls dangling between your breasts," he replied. "One way or another, I'm going to make you forget every lover you ever had, Sophie Melville."

"You're doing an excellent job of it, Jason," she approved warmly. "I can honestly tell you there's never been anyone like you in my whole life."

"That's because we're perfect together," he said.

"I think you could be right about that," she agreed.

"I am right," he insisted. "Take my word for it. There's no point in looking any further. What we've got is too special to give up."

Sophie decided that Jason's judgement was improving in leaps and bounds. She gave him every encouragement to regard the future in terms of their continued togetherness. She found that wearing black pearls and nothing else lifted lovemaking to erotic heights that she had never experienced before.

"You have very exciting visions, Jason," she told him afterwards.

"I have other visions, as well," he murmured darkly.

"Tell me about them," Sophie eagerly invited.

"I don't think you're ready for them yet."

"Why not?"

"Are your parents divorced?"

"No."

"Have they had a rotten marriage?"

"I don't think so. I suppose they've had their ups and downs, but they're still together."

"Have you any brothers and sisters?" Jason asked.

"Two older brothers."

"Married?"

"Yes."

"Are they unhappy?"

"No. They both seem happily settled. Why?"

"What about friends?" he persisted. "Any messy divorces there?"

"No."

He frowned.

"What are you getting at, Jason?" Sophie asked innocently.

"Can't you see that this flitting from man to man can only end in a very empty life?" he demanded critically. "You don't build anything solid or worthwhile if you don't stay still long enough to put down roots."

"You think I should try staying still for a while?"

His arms came around her very tightly. "Yes, I do. Wouldn't you like to have a dependable support? Someone you can always share everything with?"

"That certainly sounds nice," Sophie said consideringly, barely controlling the song of exultation in her heart.

"Think about it," Jason commanded.

Sophie had been thinking of it from the first day she'd met Jason Lombard, but she didn't think it would be strategic to enlighten him about that when he was using all his advocacy skills to win his case. After all, his pride could be stung that she had single-handedly solved the Sullivan wrangle. He might need to feel that he had won her over to the idea of marriage with him.

Jason carefully refrained from pushing the matter any further. He concentrated his full attention on showing Sophie he could fulfil all her needs. He took her to lovely places. He insisted she could let her hair down with him any time, doing or saying or expressing whatever came into her head or heart. He eagerly provided every form of support she could possibly want.

Inevitably they had to fly back to Australia, but the trip home was in vast contrast to their outward flight to Tahiti. There was love and mutual understanding in every smile, and a warm security in the way Jason continually sought to enfold her hand in his. They enjoyed the movie together and slept side by side in happy contentment.

They landed in Sydney on Sunday morning. When they walked into the airport terminal they saw newspaper posters brandishing the story of the Sullivans' reconciliation and second honeymoon. Love Not War, was the popular caption. Jason, however, was not interested in what had been printed. He hurried Sophie to the car park and became quite tense as he drove her home to Lindfield.

"Back to work tomorrow," he remarked unnecessarily.

"Yes," Sophie agreed on a sigh. "Thank you for giving me such a wonderful time, Jason. I've never been so happy with anyone."

"There's no reason why we shouldn't continue being happy together, Sophie," he said, shooting her a determined look.

"I hope we do," she said fervently.

"Then you won't mind settling up your other affairs today."

"What other affairs?" Sophie was so dizzily in love with him that she didn't understand why he frowned at her.

"The men you've been playing around with," he said tersely.

"Oh! Those!"

"You won't want them hanging around anymore."

"No. Only you, Jason."

"So make that clear to them today."

"I don't want to look at another man again," she said, giving him a dazzling smile.

He relaxed with an air of satisfaction. "I'll pick you up for work tomorrow morning."

"I'd like that."

"Then we'll talk about where we go from here," he said decisively.

Sophie smiled to herself. Jason definitely had a scheme for the future. She could feel him plotting it right down to the last move. He had a fine logical mind, and she thoroughly approved of all his tactics so far. It was nice to be able to respect and admire as well as love the man she was going to marry.

Mia was not at home when Jason carried Sophie's luggage up to the flat. However, he did not linger over kissing Sophie goodbye. He reminded her that she had things to do and left her to follow through on her promise to detach herself from all other men.

Mia came whirling into the flat ten minutes later, shrieking excitedly as she hurled her arms around Sophie and hugged her. "You got him! You got him!"

"What are you talking about, Mia?" Sophie gasped when she regained breath enough to speak.

"Jason Lombard, of course. I was walking back from the news agency, reading about Randy and Gail. And hey! Weren't we right about plonking them down on an island together?"

"It certainly helped," Sophie conceded.

"Then I ran into him outside."

"Jason?"

"And he asked me, right out of the blue, if I had some prejudice against marriage!"

Sophie grinned. "He thinks I have."

"Whatever for?"

"It worked out that way because of the Sullivans," Sophie explained, and proceeded to give her friend the general gist of all that had happened on Bora Bora.

"Wow!" breathed Mia. "Well, I tell you, he's nailed, Sophie. He said if I really cared about you as a friend, I should put in some good words about the stability and security of marriage, and he was deadly serious about it. So I ended up assuring him I was right in his camp and would back him up all the way."

"He hasn't asked me yet," Sophie said, but her eyes sparkled with happy confidence.

"There's no question of that!" Mia crowed.

But there was the question of when, Sophie thought, and the question of how best to dispose of two fictitious lovers.

CHAPTER FOURTEEN

JASON WAS so good-humoured at the office the next day that all the staff remarked on it. They were amazed but very gratified when he and Sophie distributed little gifts to everyone. Cheryl Hughes went so far as to observe that Jason Lombard seemed like a different man, and mused out loud if someone had been teaching him to be different. Sophie made no comment, but she couldn't help smiling at the knowing wink Cheryl gave her.

Jason diligently applied himself to business throughout the morning. He was openly appreciative of all Sophie did to assist him, which generated an atmosphere of happy sharing. There were no orders given. There were requests made and advice asked for and readily taken. He couldn't resist touching her whenever she was close to him. His eyes caressed her with warm pleasure. They went out to lunch together.

"You and I make a great team, Sophie," he declared over a tasty lasagne and salad. "Efficient and effective."

"You don't find me a distraction anymore?" she asked.

"We fit together very well," he continued. "If I don't think of something, you do."

"You don't mind me leaping six steps ahead?"

"The perfect complement," he said.

Sophie beamed approval at him. "I'm glad you think so, Jason."

"I do. Which is why I think we should do some serious planning for the future."

"No more being on trial? You're offering me a permanent job with you?"

"Very permanent," he assured her. "How do you feel about that?"

"Delighted. It's the best job I've ever had. I love working with you, Jason."

"Likewise," he said, beaming approval at her. "You're the best thing that ever happened to me, Sophie."

"Really?"

"Absolutely." He paused a moment, fastened his gaze purposefully on hers, then said, "Let's get married."

Sophie choked on a piece of pasta.

"Don't be like that," he said. "Think of the positive sides. You need stability in your life, Sophie. A lot of stability. I can take care of you. Look after you. Keep you happy."

Sophie took a quick sip of water. "Do you love me, Jason?" she asked.

"Love you? I'm bewitched, besotted, completely bowled over! You're the only woman in the world for me, Sophie, and I'll love you for the rest of my life.

Just say yes and let me do it. I promise you, if you put yourself in my keeping, you'll never regret it.''

"You feel that much for me?'' she asked dazedly.

"Yes. Please say yes.''

"I've got to tell you something first,'' Sophie said warily.

"I don't care about the other men,'' he said in sweeping dismissal. "It's different with me, isn't it?''

"Yes,'' said Sophie.

"That's because it feels right, doesn't it?''

"Yes.'' She nodded fervently.

"And that's why you have to marry me. Because you won't find anyone else you feel so right with.''

"That's right,'' agreed Sophie, intensely relieved that she didn't have to go into explanations. "You're the only man in my life, Jason. The only one I've ever truly loved. Ever will love,'' she affirmed with strong conviction.

"I knew it! It just had to be!'' he said triumphantly. "So we get married.''

"You're very persuasive,'' Sophie said admiringly.

"As soon as possible.''

"Perhaps we shouldn't rush it too much. We haven't known each other very long.''

"When something is right, it's right, Sophie,'' he assured her. "But if you want to make doubly sure, let's go back to the office and consult the omens. If I throw a triple twenty and a bullseye, we get married as soon as it can be arranged.''

"Oh, no!'' she groaned. "Not the omens!''

He grinned. "We'll do it just for fun. No way in the world am I going to let you get away from me, Sophie."

When they came back from lunch, Cheryl informed them that Mrs. Whitlow had arrived to see Mr. Lombard and was awaiting him in his office.

"Good opportunity for you to meet my mother properly," Jason murmured to Sophie. "She's a fine woman."

Sophie smiled happily. "I'm sure she is."

Kathryn Whitlow was standing behind Jason's desk, staring at a couple of darts that she was weighing in her hand. The frown on her face cleared as she looked up to see Jason and Sophie together. "Oh, my dears!" she cried, radiating pleasure and excitement. "I can't tell you how happy I am about the news!"

"What news?" Jason asked.

"Now don't play coy with me, Jason," his mother chided, sweeping around the desk to give him a hug and a kiss. "I know all about it."

"About what?"

"Congratulations, darling! Didn't I say she was perfect for you? Such a lovely bright girl!" his mother gushed, then turned to Sophie, her arms flung wide, ready for another embracing. "And my dear, dear girl! How I've waited for this day! You won't mind if I kiss you, too, will you?"

Sophie was too astonished to have much choice about it. Mrs. Whitlow hugged her like a long lost daughter. "It's all right for me to call you Sophie now, isn't it? And you must call me Kathryn."

"Mother, would you mind letting us know what this exhibition of affection is all about?" Jason rasped in exasperation.

"It's no use trying to keep it to yourselves, Jason. The news is out. I heard it at the hairdressers'."

"What did you hear at the hairdressers', Mother?" Jason asked with pained patience.

"That you and Sophie are getting married, of course!" his mother announced triumphantly. "And I'm so delighted, Jason. I couldn't wait for you to tell me yourselves."

"How on earth could you hear that at the hairdressers'?" Jason demanded, looking quite put out at having his thunder stolen.

Sophie decided this was not the time to tell him what Mia did for a living. She kept her mouth firmly shut.

"Well, I did hear it there. So it must be true," his mother reasoned. "I always get the real news at the hairdressers'."

"*That* snippet of information happens to be decidedly premature," Jason snapped.

"Oh!" His mother looked crestfallen.

Jason relented. "Sophie hasn't said yes yet."

His mother instantly brightened. She gave Sophie a smile that said she understood, then patted her son's arm. "In that case, I'll go and let you get on with it, dear. Perhaps a bended knee might help. You are a little arrogant, you know. But I'm sure Sophie's capable of sorting that out."

"Mother . . ." Jason steamed.

"All right! All right! I'm going!" She was halfway to the door when she stopped and wheeled around. "These darts!" She was still holding them in her hand. "They're very peculiar, Jason. I was having a little game while I was waiting for you...."

"Yes, Mother. Just give them back to me," Jason cut in, moving quickly to retrieve them.

"This one with the blue fin always lands in the triple twenty. It doesn't matter what you aim at...."

"Thank you, Mother. Sophie and I would like some privacy."

"And that red-finned one always hits the bullseye." She frowned at him. "They must be loaded with magnets or something. Don't you think it's time you put aside these boyhood tricks, Jason?"

"Mother!" he growled menacingly. "The door is waiting for you."

"All right!" She reached up and kissed him on the cheek. "Good luck, dear." Then she waved at Sophie. "He does have a good heart."

The door finally closed behind her.

Jason slowly swung around to face Sophie. "Did I say my mother is a fine woman?" he said sheepishly.

A smile twitched at Sophie's lips. "I think the omens have just been defrocked of all importance."

He shot her a look of appeal. "I did say it was only fun, Sophie."

"What about the day you hired me?" she reminded him. "Was it fun then, Jason?"

"Now, Sophie, if you remember, you were hauling me over the coals. Lots of fire coming from you. I was just balancing up the scales a bit." He gestured for a dismissal, then moved into sliding his arms around her. "After all, it was a dead certainty that the omens would be good, without any interference from you."

"But I didn't know that."

"Sophie." He lowered his voice to a passionate throb. "Even then I knew I didn't want to let you walk out of my life."

She plucked at his lapels, looking up at him from under her lashes. "You made it hard for me."

"You were giving me a lot of male problems, Sophie," he pleaded in defence.

"I desperately wanted the job. And to work with you."

"We do form a great team."

"Yes, we do."

"Will you marry me?"

"Tell me again how much you love me."

He did so, at extreme length and with heartfelt fervour. Then finally, his voice husky with emotion, he said, "Sophie, this is your last opportunity today. Will you or will you not marry me?"

She lifted her lashes and looked straight into his eloquently pleading eyes. "I love you, Jason," she said softly. "And the answer is yes. Yes, I will marry you. Yes."

**Relive the romance...
Harlequin and Silhouette
are proud to present**

A program of collections of three complete novels by the most requested authors with the most requested themes. Be sure to look for one volume each month with three complete novels by top name authors.

In June: **NINE MONTHS** Penny Jordan
Stella Cameron
Janice Kaiser

Three women pregnant and alone. But a lot can happen in nine months!

In July: **DADDY'S HOME** Kristin James
Naomi Horton
Mary Lynn Baxter

Daddy's Home... and his presence is long overdue!

In August: **FORGOTTEN PAST** Barbara Kaye
Pamela Browning
Nancy Martin

Do you dare to create a future if you've forgotten the past?

Available at your favorite retail outlet.

HARLEQUIN PRESENTS®

A Year DOWN UNDER

In 1993, Harlequin Presents celebrates the land down under. In September, let us take you to Sydney, Australia, in AND THEN CAME MORNING by Daphne Clair, Harlequin Presents #1586.

Amber Wynyard's career is fulfilling—she doesn't need a man to share her life. Joel Matheson agrees...Amber doesn't need just *any* man—she needs him. But can the disturbingly unconventional Australian break down her barriers? Will Amber let Joel in on the secret she's so long concealed?

Share the adventure—and the romance—of A Year Down Under!

Available this month in
A Year Down Under

THE STONE PRINCESS
by Robyn Donald
Harlequin Presents #1577
Available wherever Harlequin books are sold.